ID0934323

A Dead Man in Trieste

A DEAD MAN
IN TRIESTE

Michael Pearce

Constable • London

Constable & Robinson Ltd
3 The Lanchesters
162 Fulham Palace Road
London W6 9ER
www.constablerobinson.com

First published by Constable,
an imprint of Constable & Robinson Ltd 2004

A copy of the British Library Cataloguing in
Publication Data is available from the British Library

ISBN 1-84119-667-3

Printed and bound in the EU

Chapter One

Trieste was, so they had told him, the tinderbox of Europe: the sort of place where, at any moment, a spark might ignite the whole powder keg. And they were nearly right, only the spark came almost four years later, in 1914, and it wasn't in Trieste but just round the corner, in Sarajevo, when the assassination of the Archduke set in motion the train of events which became the First World War. Might, if things had been different, the killing of Lomax have been that spark, Seymour asked himself later? Only that was after the powder keg had exploded, and he was asking himself among the hailstorm of shells and bullets that was the Battle of the Somme, when he wasn't really in a condition to think clearly about anything.

On that earlier day, in Trieste, as he sat, newly arrived from London, in one of the cafés on the great central piazza, outside in the sun, all that was not just far away but totally unimaginable, so far beyond the reach of normal experience that you just, somehow, couldn't even think it.

What, actually, he was thinking, as he sat there sweating, still in the hot, dark suit, quite inappropriate for the Mediterranean but which, as a poor policeman from the East End of London, was the only one he had, was that this was all right.

Only three days before he had been in the grime of the East End; except that you hadn't been able to see the grime, in fact, you hadn't been able to see anything, because there had been a real old peasouper of a fog, come up from the docks along with a seawater chill which had driven him indoors and kept him stoking the coals of the police station fire. That was where he had been when his instructions came.

And now here he was, under the great blue sweep of the Mediterranean sky, basking in the sun, looking out through the trees at the end of the piazza at the liners in the bay.

'Very nice!' the Inspector had said when he had finished giving him his instructions. 'Sunshine. Palm trees. A holiday trip,' he had said enviously.

'Trieste?' said Seymour. 'Where's that?'

The Inspector had held back at this point, but eventually – 'Italy?' he hazarded.

This, although he had not known it, was fighting talk in Trieste. At the time, though, Seymour had felt relieved.

'That's all right,' he had said. 'I can manage Italian.'

'Ye-es?' said the Inspector, who had always thought there was something funny about Seymour.

Before going along to the Foreign Office to be more properly informed of his responsibilities, Seymour had taken the trouble to look Trieste up in the atlas. It was about half-way along the coast between what Seymour thought of as the top of Italy and –

Well, the Balkans. A lot of little countries, Serbia, Bosnia, Croatia, Slovenia, Montenegro, Herzegovina, who all got along like a house on fire. Actually, *exactly* like a house on fire.

Trieste, however, belonged to none of these. It was part of the Austro-Hungarian Empire, which at that time covered most of the southern half of Central Europe, reaching down to the sea at only one point: Trieste. Through Trieste much of its trade passed. The port was therefore important to the Empire; too important to let go. On the map the Empire hung poised above tiny Trieste like a great bulk about to fall. And that was pretty much how it seemed to Trieste's extraordinary diversity of inhabitants.

For that was the other thing about Trieste. Within its

small confines there were Italians and Austrians and Greeks and Serbs and Croats, Montenegrins and Maltese, Slovenians and Slovakians, Bosnians and Herzegovinians, not to mention Germans and Spanish and French. It was the point at which many different peoples met, met and rubbed together. And where they met there was friction, and where they rubbed there was always the possibility of a spark. Trieste was Europe in miniature, a place where all its peoples were pressed uncomfortably together, like gunpowder pressed into a barrel, like gunpowder awaiting a spark.

Through the trees on the westward side of the square he could see ships. There was a pier just beyond the trees with a ship tied up alongside it. He could see the name of the line. It was written twice, in German and in Italian: *Osterreicher Lloyd*, and *Lloyd Austriaco*. He had noticed that before, on his walk down from the hotel. Everything seemed to be double here.

In the café most of the people were speaking Italian. He listened idly to the conversation, trying to get used to the language again.

But this was embarrassing. He had thought he had known Italian, told them that he had. That was why they had picked him. But this was different from the Italian he knew. Odd phrases crept in from other languages: German, he could understand that, Slovenian, he could make a shot at. But *'sonababic'*? It took him some time to work out that it was English: son of a bitch. The influence of the docks, he supposed.

Seymour knew about docks. He had been born and bred not far from London's docks in the East End, had worked almost all his life, even when he had moved to the Special Branch, in London's dockland. It was where immigrant families like his tended to settle when they first came ashore. Even when they moved, later, they didn't move far.

7

They tended to stay in the East End even if they weren't working in the docks. They stayed with what they knew.

They came ashore in waves, the Jews at one time, the Poles, like his grandfather, at another. There had been others since. When you walked around the East End or went into its pubs and bars you would hear all kinds of languages. It was, although he did not know it, not so very different from Trieste.

It was a world, he thought, that, though foreign, the Foreign Office did not know. Lomax would not have known it. Maybe he would have known about it more than those people Seymour had met in the Foreign Office in London, because he was a consul and his work in Trieste would have taken him down if not into the docks, at least into the port. But he wouldn't really have known because, from what Seymour had seen, Foreign Office people lived in a world apart.

When he had gone in he had found two people sitting behind a desk, an older man and a younger one. The older one had looked at him without warmth.

'You know what this is all about, I suppose?' he said, as if he doubted it. 'Rather different, I imagine, from anything you've been used to.'

He turned to the younger man.

'In fact, so different that I really wonder – do we have to?' he asked.

'Proceed? I'm afraid so. The Minister was particularly insistent.'

'Yes, but – a policeman!'

'They're the ones who usually handle this sort of thing.'

'Yes, I know, but that's in the ordinary way. Surely this is a bit different?'

'That is, of course, why we asked for someone from the Special Branch.'

'Yes, but . . . You've never dealt with anything like this before, have you?' He turned the papers in front of him. 'Whitechapel. Is that where you have been working? Your

8

. . .' He seemed to pick up the word with tongs and look at it. '. . . beat?'

'Not "beat", exactly. In the Special Branch. But it's where I've been working. The East End generally.'

'The East End?' It was spoken almost with incredulity. He looked at the younger man. 'About as far, I imagine, as you can get from . . . well, the world he would be investigating.'

'Oh, I don't know,' said the younger man. 'Trieste, the docks.'

'You know what I mean. Our world. The world of the Foreign Office. Paris, Vienna.'

'This is just a consul.'

'It's still our world, though, isn't it? And a very different one from the one this gentleman is acquainted with. He'll be like a fish out of water. I don't know why they sent him.'

'Languages,' said the younger man. 'We stipulated languages.'

'But has he got them? What languages, in fact,' – the scepticism was evident – 'do you have?'

'French, German, Italian, Hungarian, Polish –'

'But to what level?' the man broke in. 'A few words are all very well down in . . . Whitechapel' – he spoke the word as if it was somehow unclean – 'but you'll need rather more if –'

'Actually, the level of foreign languages expertise in Whitechapel is rather high,' said Seymour, stung. 'They're all native speakers.'

The younger man laughed.

'Immigrants, you mean?' said the older man.

'Yes.'

'Hmm.' He was silent for a moment, considering. Then he said: 'And you yourself?'

'My grandfather was Polish, my mother Hungarian.'

The older man looked at the younger man again.

'Is that all right?'

'Very helpful, I would have thought.'

9

'No, I don't mean the languages.'

'When did your family come over here?' asked the younger man.

'My grandfather came in the early fifties.'

'After the Year of Revolutions?' said the younger man, amused.

'That's right.'

'With the police after him?' said the older man.

'The Czarist police, yes.'

'He was a revolutionary?'

'I think in English terms he would have counted just as a liberal. Today he votes Conservative.'

'And your father?'

'Born here. As I was.'

'Does he share your grandfather's views?'

'Which ones? The old ones?'

The man made an impatient gesture with his hand.

'He runs the family business. It's a timber business down by the docks. He doesn't have much time for politics. Take that in any sense you wish.'

The younger man laughed. The older one looked at him with irritation.

'This is important,' he said.

'It's also sixty years ago,' said the younger man.

'I know, I know. But one has to be sure. The point is,' he said to Seymour, 'this is an investigation which has to be handled with extreme sensitivity. Diplomatic sensitivity. There are currents . . . One would need to be confident that the man we send out was not going to be drawn into them . . .'

'Unlike, perhaps, the person whose death he would be investigating,' murmured the younger man.

Chapter Two

Lomax, the British Consul at Trieste, had disappeared. That much seemed to be certain, although much else wasn't. The younger man, for instance, had said he was dead.

Dead?

'It seems the most likely thing,' said the younger man, 'in the circumstances.'

'Could you tell me about the circumstances?'

'The immediate ones are that he was in the main piazza with some friends.'

'Drinking,' said the older man.

'And then?'

'He left. And hasn't been seen since.'

Seymour waited, but it looked as if nothing was going to be added.

'Is that all?'

'All?' said the older man. 'Isn't that enough?'

'No body?'

'Body!'

'Not yet,' said the younger man.

'Or anything that suggests foul play? Apart from his having disappeared?'

'This is Trieste,' said the younger man softly.

'But mightn't he have just, well, gone somewhere?'

'If you go somewhere, you usually come back,' said the younger man.

'Is it possible that he could simply have walked out?'

'Walked out?'

'On the job.'

11

'Consuls do not walk out on their job,' said the older man severely. 'At least, British ones don't.'

'I'm sorry,' said Seymour doggedly, 'but I still don't see why you should presume that he is dead.'

The younger man and the older man looked at each other. The older man sighed impatiently.

'It's the kind of man he was,' said the younger man.

'Always getting himself involved,' said the older man. 'Quite improper! For a consul.'

'And what we know of the situation out there.'

'Involved in what? What *is* the situation out there?'

The younger man hesitated.

'Hadn't that better wait until you get out there? It will all make much more sense to you then.'

'I doubt it,' said the older man.

'Oh, I think Mr Seymour will soon get a feel for things.'

'A tinderbox,' said the older man. 'An absolute tinderbox. And that's what we're sending him out into. One fool after another!'

But nothing seemed less like a tinderbox, as he sat there in the sun, looking at the sea sparkling through the trees, and watching the seagulls swoop in to pick up the crumbs beneath the tables. That morning, after he had checked in at his hotel, he had gone first to the Consulate and then to the main police station. In the police station he had been taken to see a Mr Kornbluth, who, it appeared, was the officer in charge of the case.

Kornbluth was sitting behind his desk, big, heavy, stolid, unyielding, like a great block of masonry, or, perhaps, a pile of rubble. He looked at Seymour unblinkingly. He seemed to be working something out. Then he said, haltingly, in English:

'You wished to see me?'

Seymour, going by the name, replied helpfully in German.

12

'I am from the British Consulate,' he said. 'My government' – that was a good start. He would soon get the hang of this diplomatic business – 'is anxious to know the circumstances in which the Consul disappeared.'

He waited.

Kornbluth said nothing.

'I wonder if you could tell me something?'

For a moment it appeared that Kornbluth could not, but then, almost reluctantly, he said:

'He was reported missing on Wednesday, the 23rd.'

'And?' prompted Seymour, when it seemed that Kornbluth was going to stop there.

'At 10.45 a.m.'

Was he merely obtuse? Or was he doing this deliberately? A word, a German word, rose up in Seymour's mind: *lumpen*. That's what Kornbluth was: *lumpen*.

'Could you give me some more details, please?'

'The last time he was seen was the evening before. In the Piazza Grande. He was with a bunch of layabouts.'

'Layabouts?'

'His friends.' Kornbluth's voice was heavy with disapproval.

Seymour was slightly taken aback. Layabouts? He would have to look into this.

'Always he was with them.'

'The layabouts?'

'In the piazza. Drinking.' Kornbluth shook his head. 'For a consul, it was not seemly.'

'Well, no. And that's what he was doing that evening?'

'As every evening.'

Seymour was beginning to get the picture.

'And then he left?'

'*Si.*'

'At about what time?'

'Nine thirty. Or so they say.'

He had slipped, apparently unconsciously, into Italian. Seymour followed him.

13

'Have they any idea where he might have been going?'

'They think he might have had an appointment. He kept looking at his watch.'

Now that he was speaking Italian, he seemed to talk more freely.

'I have looked in his appointments book, however, and there is no mention of any appointment there. His clerk, Koskash, knows nothing about one. I have spoken to the port officials – there could have been a boat coming in. But there wasn't. At the port they know nothing about it. Nor in the offices, nor in the banks.'

He paused.

'There is, anyway, something wrong in all this.'

'Something wrong?'

'Appointment? Business? Evening?' Kornbluth shook his head and suddenly appeared to twinkle. 'In Trieste,' he said, 'no one does any business in the evening!'

He glanced at his watch.

'Nor at lunchtime,' he said. 'How about an aperitif?'

Now that he was speaking Italian he seemed a different man.

'I'm sorry I spoke in German,' Seymour said. 'I was going by the name.'

'It *is* German,' Kornbluth said. 'Or, rather, Austrian. But that was a long time ago. My family have been here for, well, over a hundred years. Trieste born and bred, that's what I am.'

'And so you grew up speaking Italian?'

'Not Italian,' corrected Kornbluth. 'Triestino.'

'Ah!' said Seymour. 'That's it! I'd been wondering why it was different.'

'And the difference is important,' said Kornbluth. He looked at Seymour curiously. 'You can hear it? You speak Italian very well.'

'But not Triestino,' said Seymour.

Kornbluth clapped him on the shoulder.

'Not yet,' he said. 'But after a slivowicz or two, you will.'

He held the door open. 'We'll go down to the old city,' he

said, 'and I'll tell you something about Trieste. And about Signor Lomax.'

The Canal Grande ran back from the bay in a long three-hundred-yard spur right into the heart of the city. At the end was a domed church with a classical portico. Between the Ionic columns girls were sitting darning socks and cutting out material for cloaks. Both sides of the canal were lined with working sailing boats from which singleted crewmen were unloading sacks on to the quay. Occasionally the sacks were torn and Seymour could see what they contained: olives, pistachio nuts, figs, muscatel raisins. Whenever the contents spilled out on to the quay they were immediately seized on by young girls who scooped them up and put them in the pocket made by lifting up the front of their dress.

As well as sacks, there were barrels, either of wine or of olive oil. There were also barrels, not sacks, of coffee beans. Seymour had seen the barrels standing outside shops. Sometimes they were open and then the pungent smell spread out across the street.

The harbour was framed by tall neo-classical buildings which rose up on each side. Kornbluth took him to a little café at the foot of one of these where the tables spread out across the quay right to the edge of the water. From where they sat they could look down into a boat piled high with watermelons. The men had stopped half-way through unloading and on the quay above was a similar stack. The ripe, almost over-ripe, smell of the melons hung over the tables.

Kornbluth looked around him with satisfaction.

'Do you know what I see here?' he said.

'Boats?' hazarded Seymour.

'Work!' said Kornbluth. 'The work that has made Trieste what it is. I like to see people working. I don't mean shoving bits of paper around. I mean really putting your back into it. Now you don't always see that down in the new docks where the large ships are. It's all cranes and

15

things. But you do see it here. And what I like about it is that it's real. Real people handling real things, olives and nuts and so forth. Watermelons,' he said, looking down into the boat. 'Not fancy people pushing bits of paper around. Ah, I know that's progress, that's what it's got to be when you're a big port, as Trieste is these days, the seventh busiest in the world, so they say. But it all started here, right here, in what was the old port, with people working their asses off.'

He sipped his slivowicz.

'And that's what I don't like about layabouts. Sitting there drinking what other people's sweat has earned.

'Sweat was what built Trieste. That, and one other thing: order. Oh, I know what you think: he's a bloody policeman and so he goes on about order. But just think what Trieste is. It's Austrians and Albanians and Italians and Croats and Slovenians – Slovenia is only five miles away, you know – and Greeks and Turks and Montenegrins and Christ knows what. Now, how are all these buggers going to live together and work together if you don't have order? They'd be at each other's throats in half a minute.

'So, order and sweat. That's made Trieste what is it. Now I love Trieste and I like it as it is. And I don't want to see it go. But go it would if some of these bastards with their half-baked ideas had their way.'

'Go?' said Seymour.

'That's what they want. Some of them.'

'Go? How can it go?'

'Like Venice. Venice was part of the Austrian Empire fifty years ago. And now it's part of Italy.'

'Well, Venice *is* part of Italy. Look at the geography.'

'So is Trieste, in some people's view of geography. The geography of those layabouts, for instance.'

'The ones Lomax was with?'

'That's right. What I've got against them is not just that they're layabouts but that they want to take my city from me.'

He looked at Seymour.

'And that's the sort of people your Consul spent his time

16

with,' he said. 'The sort of people he had for his friends!'

After they had parted, Seymour walked slowly back to the Consulate. It was getting towards noon and the heat lay heavily on the streets. Shops were closing for lunch and siesta and even when they were open there didn't seem many signs of activity. A few latecomers were still pushing through the bead curtains of the doors of the bread shops but the windows were empty. Most of the day's baking had gone. In some of the dark side streets there were sounds from the tavernas but for the most part the city had gone quiet.

When he got to the Consulate he half expected to find it closed but the clerk, Koskash, was still inside, a bread roll and an orange on the desk beside him. No, he said, he didn't go home for lunch; and he wouldn't have done that anyway, in the circumstances and knowing that Seymour was here.

He was a thin, grey-haired, anxious-looking man. When Seymour had gone in that morning he had got to his feet and bowed in the Continental fashion. There was an air of formal, old-fashioned politeness about him. Like almost everyone Seymour had met, he seemed to speak several languages, switching easily from Italian to English to German. Going by his name, his home language was none of these.

It had been a distressing, sad time, he said. He and Signor Lomax had worked closely together. He had developed a great esteem for the Signor, had always found him very *simpatico*. It had been a great shock when –

Signor Seymour would find everything in order, though. There was, truthfully, not a lot of business coming into the office at the moment and what there was was all routine. He, Koskash, could handle it. Indeed, he normally did handle it. Signor Lomax left most things to him, concentrating on the occasional necessary negotiations that were the usual feature of a port consul's job. He would drop in

17

at the Consulate every morning to see how things were going and to check on what had to be done, but after that would go on down to the piazza.

Down to the piazza? Well, that was where he liked to spend the day. He was, the clerk explained, very much an 'al fresco' consul.

Fresh air consul? What was that?

The clerk hesitated.

Well, it was just that he liked to spend the day there. Usually in the Caffé degli Specchi, the Café of Mirrors. Always in the same place, at the same table.

With the same people?

Was it imagination or did Koskash shift uneasily?

Usually with the same people, yes. The artists.

Artists?

Signor Lomax was interested in art. Surely Signor Seymour had noticed the paintings in his room?

Signor Seymour had not, but he went to take a look now. How had he missed them when Koskash had shown him into the room that morning? The walls were a blaze of colour. On second thoughts he could see how he had missed them. He had looked away. They were such a blaze of colour that they quite hurt the eye. Unfortunately, there didn't seem to be much else. They weren't of anything and there didn't seem to be any pattern or shape to them.

'In Trieste,' said Koskash diffidently, 'there are many artists. There is something new here, they say. In the world of art. But I'm afraid I don't really know . . .'

And nor, certainly, did Seymour. There wasn't much call for art in the East End. Artists, there were occasionally, taking advantage of the cheap housing, but somehow he had never seen their pictures. He wouldn't have known what to make of them if he had. He felt uncomfortable with art, as he did with anything that required you to show your feelings. In Seymour's hard, tight little world of the police and the docks feeling was something you kept quiet about.

On a small table set back against one of the walls was a pile of scrap metal. There were cogs, bearings, a kind of

18

collar and a small shaft. It could have been a boat engine stripped down. But, no, Seymour was no engineer but even he could see that the bits didn't fit together. It was just a pile of scrap. Strange place to put it. Or – wait a minute – was it . . .? Could it, too, he wondered uneasily, be Art?

He closed the door and returned to the main office. One thing was already becoming clear: Lomax was a bit of an odd bloke.

Koskash had suggested several places where Seymour might go for lunch.

'A sandwich and a drink is all I need,' said Seymour.

'Then why not go down to the piazza? It is nice there. You can see the sea and there is always a little breeze.'

And it would give him a chance, thought Seymour, to meet some of Lomax's friends: those friends whom Kornbluth had thought so unsuitable and whom he had thought it important to let Seymour know about.

And so he had gone down to the Piazza Grande, and found the Caffé degli Specchi, the Café of Mirrors, and now he was sitting at the table at which, Koskash had told him, Lomax used to sit: the table he had sat at and left on the evening that he had disappeared.

A man came up, saw him at the table, hesitated and then sat down at the next table. After a while he caught Seymour's eye and raised his glass.

'You are English?'

'That's right.'

'This is your first visit to Trieste?'

'Yes.'

'There is much here to see.'

'Yes. Although actually you could say that I am here on business. There is someone whom I was hoping to meet.'

'Ah!' The man sipped from his glass. 'You are waiting, perhaps, for Lomax?'

19

'Perhaps.'
He took another sip and then put the glass down.
'Lomax won't be coming,' he said.

'So I gather.'
'You know?'
'Only a little. Really, only that he has disappeared.'
'It was last Tuesday. He had been here. Here, at this very table! Earlier in the evening. We only found out the next day. When he didn't come, we wondered. You know, he was so regular. He always used to be here. It was his place. The best place on earth, he said. He said that at last he had found his niche. So when he didn't come we thought that perhaps he was ill. A touch of malaria or something. So Lorenzo called in at the Consulate on his way home. And then he found . . .'
'He found?'
'Well, that Signor Lomax had disappeared.'
'But surely –'
'I know, I know. But he was always so regular. Say what you will, he never missed an appointment. So when he did, Koskash was worried. He went to his apartment. Lomax hadn't been there at all that night, he hadn't come home. Well, Koskash was surprised. And not just surprised, concerned. It might be nothing, but . . . So he dropped in at the police station and had a word with Kornbluth.'
'Kornbluth?'
'The Inspector. Everyone knows Kornbluth. He's a pain in the ass but he's all right, really. He said not to bother. Lomax was probably just having a lie-in with some woman. Come back if he didn't show up. Well, he didn't show up and Koskash did go back. And then . . .'
'Then?'
'You know Trieste? No? Well, in Trieste, my friend, there are two sorts of police. There are the *lamparetti*, Kornbluth's sort, the municipal guard I suppose you would call them. And then there's another sort. You understand?

20

Well, you will if you stay in Trieste any length of time. They are everywhere. Anyway, somehow they got to hear about it, and then – Jesus!

'The next moment they're all over the place. An official! An official has disappeared! Not only that, a foreign official! This is serious. If you or I disappear, my friend, that is nothing. But an official! Officials are important in Trieste. Where will it end if officials start disappearing? What will become of the Empire? And so the next moment the secret police are all over the place.'

He looked at his watch.

'And so this lunchtime everyone is late. They are probably all at the police station.'

A man came hurrying up, coat tails flying, shirt collar undone.

'Alfredo, Alfredo!'

'Lorenzo!'

They embraced warmly.

'Alfredo, I have been in prison!'

'You have been there before, Lorenzo.'

'But this time they shouted at me, Alfredo!'

'You need a drink.'

The waiter put a bottle on the table and then, without asking, half a dozen glasses.

'Where are the rest of you?'

'They are in prison, Giuseppi.'

'There must be something right that they have done, then,' said the waiter.

He poured out some wine for Alfredo and Lorenzo and was about to pour some for Seymour but then hesitated.

'Yes, yes!' cried Alfredo. 'Some for my friend!'

'Your pardon!' cried Lorenzo, noticing Seymour for the first time. He jumped up and threw his arms around him.

'A friend of Lomax's,' Alfredo explained.

'Any friend of Lomax is a friend of mine!' declared Lorenzo dramatically.

21

They drank each other's health.

Lorenzo sobered as quickly as he had fired up.

'Poor Lomax!' he said.

'Is it poor Lomax?' asked Seymour. 'Surely, it is only that he has disappeared? Might there not be some happy explanation? Couldn't he have just . . . well, gone away for a day or two?'

'Lomax never goes away.'

'But, perhaps, a sudden call of business?'

'Lomax has no sudden calls of business,' said Alfredo.

'Anyway,' said Lorenzo, 'this is where he does his business. Here!'

Two people came towards them through the tables.

'Ah! Here is Luigi! And Marinetti.'

'The bastards! They made me take my trousers down!'

'Are you sure it was the police station you went to, Luigi? There is a place down by the docks . . .'

'There is nothing to choose between the two,' said Marinetti. 'The police are all whores.'

'Yes, but they shouldn't have treated me like that. Who do they think they are? Who do they think *we* are?'

'They think we're just a bunch of Italian layabouts,' said Alfredo.

'Well, we *are* just a bunch of Italian layabouts,' said Lorenzo.

'I am not a layabout,' said Marinetti, taking umbrage.

'No?'

'No! I am an artist. And that is important. Artists are the voice of the future. But that's just the trouble. Those bastards are the voice of the past.'

'That must be why they've got it in for me,' said Luigi, sighing.

'Are you all artists?' asked Seymour. The paintings in Lomax's room were beginning to make some sense now.

'In a manner of speaking,' said Alfredo.

'No,' said Lorenzo.

'Sometimes,' said Luigi.

'Every man is an artist,' said Marinetti. 'Every man has

the capacity to create. Except for the members of the Hapsburg police.'

Alfredo looked at his watch.

'Where is Maddalena?' he fretted. 'And James?'

'Still at the police station, I expect,' said Lorenzo.

'I do not like that,' said Luigi. 'I worry when they have got her on her own.'

'If Lomax had been here, we could have asked him to see what was happening.'

There was a little silence.

'This is a friend of Lomax,' said Alfredo, remembering suddenly that he had not introduced him.

'Ah, a friend?' They shook hands. 'You have come to collect his belongings?'

'No, no,' said Seymour hurriedly. 'I didn't know until I had got here. It was a great shock.'

Lorenzo touched him sympathetically on the shoulder.

'I am here on business,' said Seymour. 'I was going to deliver something to him.'

'There is a clerk. Koskash.'

'Yes, I've met him. Most helpful. However, I think I'd better wait until I get instructions from London.'

'While you are here,' said Alfredo, 'make this your home.'

Seymour was drawn to them. He couldn't help wondering, however, if these were the kind of friends a British Consul usually had.

An hour or so later he got up, shook hands all round, and left. The artists showed every sign of staying where they were.

Seymour went back to the Consulate.

The worried-looking clerk, Koskash, was still there, bent over his desk. Evidently, siestas were not for him. Seymour wondered how far he could take him into his confidence. So far he had not told him he was a policeman, merely said that he was here to enquire into the circumstances in which Lomax had gone missing. Koskash had, of course, guessed.

23

But perhaps they ought to agree on the question of Seymour's formal status here. That seemed a suitable Foreign Office thing to do.

When he had discussed this at the Foreign Office he had found that there was considerable reluctance about him going out openly as a police officer. Might it not send the wrong signals? Imply scepticism about the ability of the local authorities to carry out a proper investigation? Suggest, too, to Vienna that London attached the wrong level of significance to the affair, more importance than Lomax, dead or living, merited? From Seymour's point of view, too, they suggested, there could be advantages in going incognito.

But then what was he to go as? There was a long discussion about this, longer, in fact, than there had been about Lomax himself and his disappearance. The older man ruled out Seymour's trying to pass as a diplomat, however junior. It was quite unthinkable. A manservant, perhaps? The younger man doubted whether Lomax had gone in for menservants. He was, after all, only a consul. A Consulate guard, then? Wasn't it a little late for that, asked the younger man. And mightn't that be to attach too little significance to the role? How would it look to the Minister?

In the end it was agreed that Seymour should go out to Trieste as a King's Messenger, which sounded appropriately superior but was appropriately inferior.

Koskash listened carefully but looked doubtful.

'We haven't had a King's Messenger here before,' he said hesitantly. 'Usually they just go to the embassies.'

'Perhaps, then, no one here will know quite what to expect,' said Seymour, 'and that might be all to the good.'

Koskash continued to look doubtful but since it had already been determined, he had no alternative but to acquiesce.

'What did you tell Kornbluth?'

'Merely that I was from the Foreign Office and that

London wanted to know about the circumstances surrounding Lomax's disappearance.'

Koskash nodded.

'All right so far,' he said; but there was still a note of doubt in his voice.

Seymour went on through into Lomax's room. Apart from the pictures it was sparsely furnished. There was just a desk and a few chairs. Files, presumably, were kept outside in Koskash's room.

Seymour sat down at the desk and went through the drawers. They were practically empty. In one of them, stuffed away without interest, was a list of diplomatic representatives in the area, but that was all. On top of the desk were an in-tray and an out-tray, both empty. There was also an appointments book. That was empty, too.

The room felt as if it hadn't been inhabited for a long time. Perhaps it hadn't been, if Koskash hadn't been exaggerating when he had said that Lomax spent all his time down in the piazza. But if that was the case, then where had he done his work? If, that was, he had done any.

Later in the afternoon Seymour got a key from Koskash and went to Lomax's apartment. It was in a large, crumbling house. The rooms were high and dark, but that made them cool, a thing to be sought after in Trieste in the summer. For the same reason, perhaps, the furniture was mostly wickerwork. Again there wasn't much of it: one or two chairs, a small table and a dressing-table. It looked as if Lomax hadn't spent much time here, either.

In the bedroom there was a wardrobe with a few suits. Seymour went through the pockets and found only a letter from an Auntie Vi who lived in Warrington and a surprising number of ticket stubs. The bed was a large wooden one with a single sheet and a Continental bolster-like pillow. When Seymour bent over it he caught a faint whiff of a woman's perfume.

Afterwards Seymour went back to the Consulate. Koskash

25

had gone now and Seymour sat at his desk, in the darkening room, thinking.

He didn't know what he had expected to find but this wasn't it. He had been sent out to Trieste to find a man or at least to find out what had happened to him. But he hadn't found a man, either here or in the apartment. Where was Lomax's life?

In the piazza, apparently. That was what Koskash had said, what Kornbluth had said, and what the artists had said and Seymour seemed to have no choice now other than to accept it.

But . . .

This was a consul, after all. Was that how consuls usually spent their time? One part of Seymour would have liked to think it; but the other part, the strict, conventional part which came originally from his family's strongly Puritanical background on the Continent and then from two generations of life as a new immigrant, with all its pressures to keep your head down and not stand out, to make yourself invisible by observing the norms of your adopted society and becoming more English than the English, was faintly shocked.

Seymour was at heart a bit of a conformist; and Lomax didn't seem to conform at all! How did that play in London, Seymour wondered? Not very well, if his own experience at the Foreign Office was anything to go by. And not very well with officialdom in Trieste, either, judging by what Kornbluth had said.

But Kornbluth had said something else, too, or, at least, had hinted at it. He had gone out of his way to link Lomax with that strange group of artists and the artists with . . . what? Nationalistic activity of some sort? Political trouble-making? Had Lomax allowed his sympathies to run away with him and identified himself too closely with their preoccupations? And had that had something to do with his disappearance? Or death? Was that what Kornbluth had been hinting?

And was that, too, what those men at the Foreign Office, in their obscure, supercilious way, had been suggesting?

26

Were those the currents that they feared Lomax had allowed himself to be drawn into?

Later, Seymour walked down to the piazza. The lamps in the cafés were coming on. The tables were filling up. The space in the middle of the piazza, which had been empty when Seymour had been there earlier in the day, was now crowded with people. There were whole families, grandparents, parents and children, the children running on ahead or pushing themselves after on wheeled wooden horses, all out together; there were young girls arm in arm, young men, always apart from the girls, usually in groups, older couples turning aside from time to time to chat to people they recognized at the tables. There were uniforms everywhere. Was this a garrison town? But they didn't look like soldiers. And then he suddenly realized what they were. Officials. Alfredo had said that there were a lot of officials in Trieste, and hadn't Seymour read somewhere that in the Empire all officials, from the topmost civil servant to the bottom-most postman or clerk, wore uniforms?

They were all walking in the same direction towards the seaward end of the huge piazza, where the lamps in the trees around the bandstand had come on too, and where, beyond the trees, rows of little lights indicated the positions of the liners in the bay.

And suddenly Seymour knew what this was. The word came floating up in his mind: the *passeggiatta*, that great Mediterranean ritual, the evening stroll to take the air.

Seymour had learnt the word from old Angelinetti, standing in the doorway of his shop back in the East End, looking out mournfully on the grey-green fog which came up from the docks every evening at that time of year. He had spat out the taste and then told Seymour, the young Seymour, about the *passeggiatta*. Seymour had caught some of the feeling that the word contained, the sense of release after the work and heat of the day, the communal taking of

27

pleasure. Now his own experience caught up with the word.

Almost despite himself, despite his English stiffness, he felt a kind of inner easing. Had Lomax, too, he wondered, felt an easing when he came to Trieste? Some sort of reaction, perhaps, against the constraint and formality of life in the Foreign Office? Was that what had led him to stepping over the traces? If over the traces he had stepped.

The artists were still at the table. He hesitated a moment and then approached them. At once he was hauled into their circle, welcomed with embraces, plied with wine. He felt his reserve – and Seymour had plenty of reserve – melting.

A puff of wind came up from the sea front. It smelt of flowers and of the sea. In the bandstand the band was playing a waltz and beneath the trees people were dancing. Seymour could see bright dresses and the flash of gilt from the uniforms. He thought that perhaps he should go back to his hotel but found it difficult to move.

'It will be big,' Marinetti was saying.

He seemed to be talking about some event that he was organizing.

'And noisy,' he added with satisfaction.

'Will there be drink?' asked Lorenzo.

'Oceans!'

'Who's paying?' asked Alfredo.

Marinetti frowned.

'There are some details yet to be settled,' he said.

There was now a counter-flow to the movement down to the sea front. People had begun to make their way back. They dropped off into the cafés or into the side streets. Several turned aside to greet the group at Seymour's table.

'No James tonight?' one of them said.

'Not yet. I think he's probably still at the police station,' Alfredo said.

'No, no. I saw him coming into the piazza.'

'Well, where the hell is he, then?'

Another, hearing that Seymour was Lomax's friend, came specially round the table to shake his hand.

'How can it be,' he said, 'that someone can just disappear? In a place like Trieste?'

'I'll tell you,' said Marinetti belligerently. 'In the same way as James has disappeared.'

'James has *not* disappeared –'

'And Maddalena –'

'Maddalena probably hasn't either!'

'In the same way as we're *all* going to disappear,' roared Marinetti. 'They take us in and they let us out. Then one day they take us in and they don't let us out. Not ever! Ever!'

He burst into tears.

'Poor Lomax! The bastards!'

He collapsed, sobbing, across the table.

'I think perhaps I'll –' began Seymour, starting to get up.

The others sprang up, too.

'Your hotel –'

'Do you know the way?'

'We'll show you –'

'It's all right, thanks.'

'No, no! We'll come with you.'

They all got up, apart from Marinetti, and began to accompany him across the piazza. As they were turning off into one of the side streets, they nearly tripped over someone lying drunk in the middle of the road.

'Why, it's James!' Lorenzo said.

Chapter Three

Seymour was used to covert operations and that, he told himself, was all this was. But this was very different. In the East End he had been part of a team and there had been a certain sharing of information. Here he was on his own and although Kornbluth had promised to keep him informed he knew he could not rely on that in the same way. Yet Kornbluth was the man conducting the investigation and there were things he could do that Seymour couldn't. He could openly question witnesses, for example, or people who might have witnessed something: Lomax leaving the piazza, for instance. But any information that Seymour gleaned would have to be gathered indirectly.

He was already beginning to find it frustrating. In England if he was starting on a case there were obvious things he would have done. Here he could do none of them. He would have to wait for Kornbluth to do them and then hope that he would tell Seymour about it afterwards. How did you begin if you were having to operate covertly but without the larger operation around you?

But perhaps he was being too impatient. What was it that the two men at the Foreign Office had said? That they had had doubts about Lomax because of the kind of man he was: and they had been afraid that he would involve himself too readily in 'the situation' out there in Trieste. Perhaps he ought to start there and, for the moment, leave what happened on the night that Lomax had disappeared to Kornbluth.

So far he hadn't got much of a picture of Lomax the man

and why he had seemed frankly out of place. There must be more to Lomax than that. He *must*, for a start, have done some work.

Oh, yes, said Koskash, slightly offended, Signor Lomax was very conscientious. He would never, he insisted, neglect his work.

What was this work? Well, of course, most of it was to do with the port. There were always English ships coming in and sometimes they had problems or they needed help with the paperwork. Or perhaps there was some problem with Customs or with the Port Authority which required Lomax to go down and sort things out. He was very good at that, Koskash said.

Seymour was relieved to hear it. Up till then he had been getting the impression that Lomax's day consisted largely of sitting around and drinking.

No, no, said Koskash, or, at least, not entirely. That was where he sat, his base, as it were, where people always knew they could find him. After he had been down to the port, or wherever, he would come back there and that was where people would go if they needed his help. A little odd, perhaps, but this was Trieste and the Mediterranean and a lot of things were conducted outside, al fresco, so why shouldn't a consul be al fresco too?

Why not, thought Seymour? Or a policeman. It seemed a good idea. But what exactly would people be coming to see him about? Could Koskash give an example?

Certainly, said Koskash obligingly. Take seamen, for instance. They were always coming to the Consulate for loans. They would be paid off at the end of the voyage and then spend all their pay in the tavernas or brothels. And then they would come to the Consul for a loan until they signed on again.

'And he would give it them?' said Seymour incredulously.

'We would recover it when they signed on again. It was just a temporary loan. They would come to him at the café and he would make out an order to pay. Then they would

31

bring it to me and I would pay them. Look, I will show you.'

He went away and came back with a pile of slips of paper.

'But these are all bills from the Caffé degli Specchi!'

'No, no.' He turned them over. On the back of each one was written 'Order to Pay' and then a sum, together with a name, and Lomax's signature.

'Are you sure you didn't pay for anything on the other side?' said Seymour suspiciously.

'Certainly not!' Koskash was offended. 'I would never do a thing like that. It would be quite improper.'

'Well, yes, but would you call this' – he held out a handful of bills – 'exactly proper?'

'It is unusual, I admit. But as an accounting system it is certainly proper. An order to pay for every payment. No payment without an order to pay – you can check the cash ledger if you like. The books are all in order.'

Seymour checked them. They were.

'It's hardly usual,' he said weakly, handing the books back.

'Well, no, and I was very concerned about it at first, when Signor Lomax introduced the system. But I had to admit that, accounting-wise, there was nothing wrong with it. And in fact it seemed to work very well.'

Seymour made a mental note to check Lomax's bank account and see if Lomax's talent for creative accounting extended further.

As Koskash began to gather up the slips of paper, Seymour turned them over and looked at the other side.

'These sums are quite sizeable. If you are sure you didn't pay, who did? Lomax?'

'You can't tell from the bills,' said Koskash, 'but I think that, as a matter of fact, he often did.'

That brought up another issue. What exactly was Lomax's relationship to the artists? He was interested in art, yes, the pictures on the walls of his room were evidence of that. But he hardly spent any time in his room so possibly he didn't look at them much. Wasn't that odd, if he loved art so much?

Another thought, prompted by the sight of the bills, struck Seymour. Was Lomax, for some reason, their financial provider? Was that why he had bought the pictures? And was that why he had contributed, so generously, apparently, to their drinking bills?

But if he was their financier, then why? Love of art? Or was there some other reason? As, perhaps, Kornbluth had suggested.

'These artists,' he said: 'can you tell me something about them?'

Koskash shrugged.

'We have a lot of artists in Trieste,' he said. 'And people who think they are artists.'

'And which category do these fall into?'

'Marinetti is good. Preposterous, but good.'

'And the others?'

'I don't know. It doesn't mean anything to me.'

'But it did to Lomax?'

Koskash hesitated.

'I don't know how much it meant to him really. He didn't seem to have this enthusiasm when he came. But then he suddenly developed it.'

'After he met the artists or before?'

'After he met Maddalena,' said Koskash drily.

'Maddalena? I've come across her name before.'

'She hangs out with the artists. I think she acts as a model for them.'

'And she introduced him to them?'

'Or vice versa, I can't remember which. But suddenly she was very important, and so was art.'

Well, it was another bit of the picture he was getting of Lomax: drinking, idling – all this al fresco stuff – and now sex! Seymour was hardly surprised that one day he had simply disappeared. It seemed in keeping.

But then there was this other side, this possible involvement in 'currents', the possibility that he had not wandered off but been killed.

'What about these artists?' he said. 'What sort of people are they?'

Koskash shrugged.

'Well,' he said, 'they're artists. They don't always behave like other people.'

'They seemed to me, when I was speaking to them, to have got across the authorities.'

'Yes,' said Koskash. 'They have a talent for that.'

'Kornbluth seemed very down on them. With justification, do you think?'

'That depends on how you see it,' said Koskash cautiously.

'Kornbluth seemed to see them as troublemakers. Political troublemakers.'

'Political?'

'Nationalist.'

'Listen,' said Koskash, 'in Trieste, *everyone* is a nationalist.'

It ought to be easy to find that out, thought Seymour. The artists didn't seem to hold things back. But then there was the question of Lomax's own sympathies and how far he had allowed them to carry him. It might even be possible to find that out from them too. Or maybe he could talk to that girl.

He wasn't altogether happy, though, about the direction in which his enquiries were leading him. In the Special Branch there was a political side and that was, in fact, the side to which he had naturally gravitated. Or, rather, his superiors had gravitated him, chiefly, he suspected, on the grounds that he was 'languages' and languages were foreign and political trouble – in their possibly not unprejudiced view – tended to come from foreigners. In the East End, with its high proportion of political refugees, it prob-

34

ably did come from 'foreigners'; but, then, since there were
so many 'foreigners' in the East End, that was true of the
rest of the crime as well.

Seymour had never been entirely happy about his drift
towards that side of the Branch's activities. Partly that was
because of his family's unhappiness. With their history of
falling foul of the police in their original countries, they
hadn't been happy about him joining the police at all. But
to go into the Special Branch, and on to the political side,
which was the side that tended to impact on them, seemed
to them the heights, or depths, of eccentricity.

But Seymour had his own reservations, too. Some of
these were psychological, the traditional immigrant dis-
trust of getting involved in politics; but others were to do
with principle. He retained sufficient of his family's res-
tiveness under government to feel uneasy about working
for government himself. It was an issue he had still not
resolved, was still debating with himself.

Now here it was coming up again and in a form which
had a particular acuteness for him. From what Kornbluth
had hinted, there was a possibility that the currents Lomax
had got himself involved with were nationalist ones.

Nationalism, as it happened, was big in the Seymour
household. Too big, and Seymour had always tried to steer
clear of it. It was his grandfather's over-enthusiasm for
nationalism that had led to his having to leave Poland in
a hurry. At least he had got out. Seymour's other grandfather, in a different country, had not been so lucky. Seymour's father had, partly in consequence, reacted strongly
against politics in general and nationalist ones in particular, and Seymour had tended to follow him. Now here the
issue was again coming back to haunt him.

Seymour was able to clear up one other point to do with
Lomax's work: his empty appointments book.

'He never used it,' said Koskash.

'What did he use?'

35

He might have guessed it.

Slips of paper.

'I kept a separate book,' said Koskash, 'and would give him notes for the day.'

Seymour thought he might have seen one in one of Lomax's suits.

'Rough scraps of paper?'

'They didn't start like that,' said Koskash, pained.

Seymour sighed.

'What had he got against ordinary paperwork?'

'He said it was on the side of government.'

'On the side of *government*?'

What was it with this man? Was he some kind of anarchist?

'He said that it was paper that made bureaucracy possible and that there was too much bureaucracy in the world. In Trieste,' said Koskash drily, 'such a view is distinctly unusual.'

From the separate book which Koskash had kept Seymour was able to reconstruct Lomax's movements in the week that he had disappeared. As Koskash had said, they consisted largely of visits to the Port Authority or to the docks. The one exception was a visit to the Casa Revoltella.

'Casa Revoltella?' said Seymour. 'What was that?'

'It was a civic reception. A big one, the Governor was there. All the consuls were invited. The Casa Revoltella is a house in the Piazza Giuseppina. It used to belong to the Baron Revoltella. He left it to the city when he died. You should go there. You would find it interesting. You would see how the rich in Trieste used to live. And still live, for that matter.'

The house was open to the public and that afternoon, when the city was quiet, Seymour went there. It was, as Koskash had said, an excellent example of the way of life of the old Trieste merchant, with velvet red plush and gilt everywhere. The Baron Revoltella had been one of those who had spotted the significance to Trieste of the opening of the Suez Canal. The Canal's third entrance, they called Trieste.

The house was full of reminders of the Suez connection, from broad canvases of the Canal itself to a very strange piece of art on the stairs called *Cutting the Isthmus*, which had a plaque of de Lesseps on one side of its plinth and a plaque of the Khedive Abbas on the other. The whole thing was lit up from time to time by a red bulb held in the fangs of a wrought-iron serpent.

Money dripped from the large gilt chandeliers and showed itself in the thick pile of the carpet on the velvet-railed staircase up which, presumably, the guests had mounted a fortnight ago.

Seymour asked the attendant about the reception. It appeared to have been a splendid occasion, graced by the Governor himself, and at which almost all the commercial and official worthies of the city had been present.

'The flower of the city,' said the attendant sentimentally.

And among the flowers, the dandelion, perhaps, in the bouquet, had been Lomax. All the consuls, the attendant assured him, had been present. He produced some photographs of the occasion: of wondrously uniformed men and gorgeously dressed ladies, sashed and fanned. Seymour wondered if Lomax had worn a uniform, too. Did consuls have uniforms? He suspected they did. Especially if they were British.

He wondered, too, how he had felt. Because he would not, surely, have fitted in. The superior people Seymour had encountered at the Foreign Office, yes, they would have fitted in. But Lomax? From what Seymour felt he had learned about him he would have gone with reluctance, arriving late and leaving early, knowing the people, perhaps, but less at ease in these formal surroundings than in the relaxed atmosphere of the café tables. Seymour looked for him in the photographs, asking the attendant to point him out, but they couldn't find him. He was, as ever, the missing man.

In one of the rooms was a large telescope trained on the bay, through which the Baron could watch his ships coming in. Seymour looked at the ships, too, and then idly adjusted the telescope and found himself peering down on the square outside. There was a statue in the middle of the square and a woman standing nearby. The statue – he could read the inscription through the telescope – was of the Archduke Maximilian, a fine figure, bald, bearded and, of course, this being Trieste, in uniform. The woman appeared to be working on it.

Or, just a minute, was she? She had given it a red nose, large breasts with huge red nipples, and red drawers, into the seat of which she was fitting two large balloons.

What the hell was this? Some kind of student prank?

When he came out of the Casa Revoltella the woman was still there. She had added a cigar, stuck, somehow, into the statue's mouth, and a fish, draped casually over the Duke's ear.

Amused, and slightly curious, he wandered over towards her.

She stepped back to admire her handiwork.

'For God's sake, Maddalena!' said a voice that Seymour recognized.

'Alfredo, is that you? You have come at last. Have you brought it?'

'Yes, but –'

'Please, Alfredo! What is art without the recording?'

She draped herself beside the statue while Alfredo assembled an ancient camera upon a tripod. He disappeared for a moment beneath the cloth. Then his head appeared again.

'Maddalena, is this wise?'

'I hope not.'

'No, no. That you should appear in the photograph, I mean.'

'You think that the artist should not show herself in her work but be somewhere else, indifferently paring her fingernails?'

'I was merely thinking that offering too faithful a record might be to be unnecessarily helpful to the police.'

'Perhaps you are right.'

She removed herself from the statue.

Alfredo suddenly noticed Seymour.

'Maddalena, this is a friend of mine. A friend of Lomax's too.'

She came over to him.

'A friend of Lomax's?'

'Well, not exactly a friend –'

'He has just arrived from London.'

'From London? You are a consul, too?'

'No, no. Just a King's Messenger.'

She moved away.

'Alfredo!'

'Yes?'

'You disappoint me. First, you didn't want to take my photograph, and now you are friends with kings!'

'Messenger,' said Seymour. 'Just Messenger.'

'Are you?' said Alfredo. 'You didn't tell me that.'

'You should choose your friends more carefully, Alfredo. However, since he is also a friend of Lomax's, I will forgive you this time.'

'Thank you, Maddalena. And now may I get on with taking the photograph before the policeman gets here from the next piazza?'

He put his head back beneath the cloth.

'Alfredo.'

'Yes, Maddalena?' wearily.

'A touch of mascara around his eyes, do you think?'

'No.'

'Spoiling the ship, you think?'

'I think the policeman will get here before I finish taking the photograph.'

'How do you know he is coming?'

'Because I can see him across the piazza.'

On the other side of the piazza there was a sudden shout and then a piercing blast on a whistle.

'Maddalena –'

'There is no hurry. He is very fat and will take some time to get here.'

Alfredo emerged hurriedly from beneath the cloth.

'Did you get it?'

'Of course.'

He lifted off the camera and grabbed the tripod.

'You run that way,' said Maddalena, 'and I will run the other way.'

So this was Maddalena, thought Seymour. The woman, according to Koskash, who might have accounted for Lomax's sudden enthusiasm for art and who had, perhaps, introduced him to the artists. Well, from what he had so far learned about him, she fitted pretty well with the picture of Lomax that Seymour was beginning to build up. An oddball woman to go with an oddball man.

He could quite see, however, how a woman like Maddalena might appeal to a man like Lomax. He constructed for himself a mental picture of a staid single man who had spent all his life as a conventional diplomat and who had then, suddenly, run into a woman who was completely outside his range of experience, striking – she was beautiful, Seymour suddenly realized, in an odd, offbeat kind of way, he could quite see how an artist might want her to model for him – unconventional, disturbingly so, challenging Lomax (excitingly?) in all his conventional pores, vital – vital enough, perhaps, to pour new blood into a consul's shrivelled-up veins and make him fancy he could lead a new life, start again in this sunny Mediterranean place, break free from the mould, kick over the traces –

40

Run away? Walk out on a job that suddenly seemed stale and sterile to him? Run away with Maddalena and start again?

Only he hadn't run away. At least, not with Maddalena. She was still here. It was only he who had disappeared.

And maybe the whole picture was false, anyway. Maybe she had not had an impact on him quite like that. Maybe he had indeed, for a moment, entertained the fantasy, put a foot over the traces, but then the ingrained caution of the diplomat had reasserted itself, telling him that though it was lovely it was not for him.

He was going too far in his speculation, he knew. But something had happened to Lomax when he had come to Trieste. Something had changed him. (Because he couldn't have been like this before he was posted to Trieste, could he? Surely they would have kicked him out?) No, he had changed after he arrived. That was what Koskash had said, hadn't he? His passion for art hadn't been there when he arrived, it had developed afterwards, after he had met Maddalena. No, something had changed Lomax on his arrival in Trieste, and that something looked very much like Maddalena.

It was almost disappointingly simple. A single, middle-aged man, stuck in the groove for most of his life, had suddenly been jolted out of it by meeting a beautiful, disturbing woman and had stepped over the traces. It was an old story.

But was it a true one? Seymour tested it again and felt, yes, that he would go for it in every particular.

Except one. Where *was* Lomax? Set aside Kornbluth's dark hints and the Foreign Office's oblique ones, set aside speculation about currents nationalist or otherwise, and you were still left with the fact that a responsible man, a consul, had disappeared. Seymour would have to explain that, discover what had happened to him, before he could go home.

But meanwhile he could enjoy the sun and all the diverse life of a great sea port. He could listen to all the

41

different voices, of especial interest to him as a man who in a sense lived in languages. He could even hear, faintly, echoes of the languages of his childhood and of the languages of the East End and, more faintly still, echoes of the experience behind the languages.

And he might even, he almost certainly would, meet Maddalena again. Seymour was no Lomax. He was, for a start, ten, fifteen, years younger. No mid-life crisis for him, not, at any rate, for some time yet. No urge to kick over the traces – he was very happy with the way things were, thank you. And there was no likelihood at all of his falling for what his mother would call a fancy woman.

All the same, at the prospect of meeting Maddalena again, he felt his pulses quicken.

That evening he went back to his hotel early to write his first report, an obligation the Foreign Office had laid upon him. Regular reports every three days. Empires, whether British or Austro-Hungarian, ran on paper. Lomax had been right about that.

He didn't find it easy. Kornbluth had been long on hints and short on the particulars of Lomax's disappearance and Seymour knew little more now than he had when he arrived. And how far should he set down the details of Lomax's al fresco style as Consul? Even to remark it might seem to the lordly people of the Foreign Office like . . . what was the phrase? *Lèse-majesté*. Taking the sovereign's majesty lightly. And then that kind of detail didn't fit too well in a formal report; not in the kind of report you wrote in Whitechapel, anyway.

In the end he kept it brief and factual, putting in the times and dates that Kornbluth had given him and confining his account of Lomax to a few vague phrases: 'slightly irregular style of life', that sort of thing. It took him a long time, however, and he didn't get to bed till late.

*   *   *

In what seemed the middle of the night he was woken by Koskash and told that he should go down to the little harbour where the fishing boats docked.

It was still dark as they went through the streets. Nothing was stirring even in the tiny piazzas where the markets were held. Seymour had half expected to find the ox-carts already coming in with their produce and no doubt they would be doing so later. He caught the raw sea smell as they drew near to the docks and felt the chill of the water on his face.

Down by the harbour there was movement. Men were already standing at the edge of the quay ready to unload the fishing boats as they came in, and in a long shed set back from the water and lit only by a dim lamp women were waiting with their knives.

A man detached himself from the dark huddle on the quayside and came towards them. It was Kornbluth. They shook hands.

'I am sorry,' he said.

Out in the bay Seymour could see lights.

'The boats are coming in,' Kornbluth said.

The lights seemed steady at first but as they drew nearer they swayed and bobbed. He saw that they were attached to the tops of the masts and moved to the movement of the sea.

It was getting lighter now and he could see more clearly the people standing waiting. Ox-carts were assembling near the shed, ready to take the fish up to the markets. Already there was a strong smell of fish in the air.

The men on the quay began to stir. The first boat was coming in.

It turned and nosed its way along the quay. Ropes were thrown and it came to a stop. Men at once jumped down into its hold.

Kornbluth went to the edge of the quay and asked something. One of the fishermen jerked his thumb over his shoulder.

The other boats were coming in now. In the growing

43

light Seymour could see their blunt prows more clearly and make out the cabbalistic symbols on their sides. As each boat tied up, Kornbluth went to it and said something. Eventually he came to one and stopped.

He came back to where Seymour and Koskash were standing and said:

'Over here.'

They went up to the shed where the women were waiting with their knives. They had spread out along a grey, stone table.

The first fish were tipped on to it and they set to work immediately. There was a lamp overhead and in its light the scales of the fish glinted. Where the lamp did not reach, the fish glowed in the darkness with a strange luminescence. Already the colours of the fish were fading.

Outside, men were loading barrels on to the carts and the first cart had already set off.

Kornbluth led them through to an inner room where there was another grey slab and some women were opening shellfish. They inserted the tips of their knives, twisted and prised the lips apart. Then, without taking the shells off, they dropped them into buckets at their feet.

Kornbluth told them to stop and they shrugged their shoulders and moved away.

Fishermen brought in a plank on which something was lying. They tipped it on to the slab.

Kornbluth said something testily and one of the men brought in another lamp, which he put down at the head of the slab.

There was a reek of fish in the air and water dripped down on to the floor. Kornbluth removed some of the seaweed and threw it into a corner. Then he took the lamp and held it up above the face of the man who was lying there. He looked at it steadily for a moment and then nodded.

Then he pulled Koskash forward and held him while he lifted the lamp and Koskash looked down.

'Yes?' he said.

Chapter Four

Seymour was sitting in Lomax's apartment. On the table in front of him was a pile of ticket stubs, the ones he had noticed in the pockets of Lomax's empty suits. He counted forty-seven of them. He knew now what they were: cinema tickets.

Cinema? Seymour knew, of course, what cinemas were. He had even been to one, once. But they didn't figure big in the East End. They didn't figure that largely, as far as he knew, in the more prosperous districts further west. The one in the East End was above a billiards room and its grey, disjointed, flickering delights were intended to add to the appeal of the room below; as well as, Seymour suspected, enticing patrons on to further rooms upstairs in which ladies were waiting to encourage them to other forms of activity. It all seemed very dubious to Seymour.

But here in Trieste cinema did not seem at all dubious! On the contrary, it seemed above board, thriving and very popular.

'There's the Excelsior, the Americano, the Edison, the Royal Biograph, the Teatro Fenice . . .' Kornbluth said with pride. 'Trieste,' he said, 'is the cinema capital of the world.'

Seymour felt slightly put out. London, in his mind, was the capital of the world in almost everything: and now to come to a place like Trieste, which, let's face it, no one had ever heard of, and find that it, too, had claims was mildly disconcerting. Of course, the claims were only to leadership in the seedy world of a dubious form of popular entertainment, but all the same . . . Seymour had already taken it for granted that the appeal of the cinema would flicker out in the same way as its jerky images were always threatening to do; or, at least, that cinema would not catch on. Could he have been wrong? Could this actually be in some way the shape of the future?

Surely not. And yet Lomax has evidently embraced it wholeheartedly. More than wholeheartedly: extravagantly. Forty-seven tickets! The man must have been completely hooked.

Another not exactly normal thing to add to the apparently infinite list of Lomax's eccentricities! But Seymour felt a little twinge of sadness. Was this all that Lomax's stepping over the traces amounted to? Was going to the cinema the summit of the *dolce vita*? If it was, Seymour felt the need for a certain revisionism in his thinking.

And yet it looked as if this mild, slightly ridiculous, excess had had a part to play in whatever it was that had happened to Lomax. For in going through the pockets of the suit that Lomax had been dressed in, in the presence of Seymour as consular representative, Kornbluth had found a grey, smudged, almost dissolved ticket, just one, but which Kornbluth, looking at it, had thought could be for a performance on the night that Lomax had died.

'I can't be sure,' he said. 'I'll have to put it to my people. But I think it's for the Edison, and they changed the tickets just about that time. This is one of the new ones.'

There was nothing that Seymour himself could do with the tickets. It would have to await the verdict of Kornbluth's people. He pushed the pile away and turned to making a list of Lomax's effects. He would send it back to London and they, presumably, would forward it on to Lomax's next of kin.

The thought sent his mind back to the letter from Lomax's 'Auntie Vi' which had also been found stuffed in

46

the pocket of one of his suits. Seymour took it out and read it through.

The big news it contained was that Lomax's Uncle Sid had gone in to Manchester to have his teeth done. Seymour knew Manchester or, rather, of Manchester. It was another place where immigrants went. Some of the Jewish tailors he knew in the East End had relatives there. What they had told him of the poorer parts where they lived had not made him want to go there.

And yet for Auntie Vi Manchester had seemed an El Dorado. While Uncle Sid had been having his teeth done she had gone to 'the big shops' and she listed their names and her purchases with starry-eyed breathlessness. Seymour wondered what Warrington could be like.

Warrington, it appeared, was where Lomax had grown up too. The letter was full of 'you will remember, of course' and references to places and people's names. Seymour wondered if Auntie Vi and Uncle Sid had been substitute parents. There was no mention of parents and the letter breathed a closeness which Seymour, used to family closeness, could recognize.

But if it breathed closeness, it also breathed narrowness. Lomax had travelled a long way to get from Warrington to Trieste. Seymour had learned enough about the Foreign Office now to realize that there was a considerable difference between a consul and the lordly figures he had encountered in London. A consul, he had worked out, was the journeyman of the Diplomatic Service, the man who conducted much of the humdrum business of ports and trade. He operated at a different level from the ambassadors and secretaries and, given the kind of institution that the Foreign Office seemed to be, that meant that he was usually recruited from a different social level. Going by the letter, that certainly seemed to be true in Lomax's case. Coming from such a background, Lomax had done well to get where he had done. Trieste, Seymour was beginning to see, was a more important place than he had thought.

He read through the letter again and was struck by its warmth. The news of Lomax's death would come as a shock. He hoped that the Foreign Office would break it gently. When he remembered the stiffness of the people he had encountered there, however, he didn't think that was likely. Prompted by a sudden movement of sympathy, arising, perhaps, because the memory of Lomax lying there on the slab was so fresh in him, he wrote Auntie Vi a letter of condolence. He realized, of course, that it was not the sort of thing he should do: either as a policeman or as a member, if only temporary, of the Diplomatic Service.

'If you or I disappear,' Alfredo had said, 'that is nothing. But if an official disappears . . .!' And all the more so, apparently, if an official died in suspicious circumstances. Nobody had taken much notice of Lomax living; dead, he seemed to have become the centre of Trieste's attention. A whole string of people came to the Consulate to express their condolences.

Mostly they expressed them to a slightly surprised Seymour.

'Well, they wouldn't express them to me,' said Koskash. 'I am just a clerk.'

'Yes, but I'm not even – I mean, I'm not a permanent person here.'

'You don't have to be permanent, you just have to be British,' said Koskash. 'And vaguely official. A uniform would, of course, help.'

'Well, I can tell you –'

'It doesn't matter,' said Koskash kindly. 'There just has to be some focus for symbolic diplomatic action. A donkey would do just as well.'

Seymour wasn't sure if this made him feel any better. Anyway, the doyen of the consular corps was waiting outside so he pulled himself to attention, put on a sombre face, and told Koskash he could show him in.

Signor Caramelli was a distinguished-looking, grey-

48

haired man who shook his hand sadly and then held on to it for longer than Seymour liked.

'It is with deep regret. . . . I speak for the whole consular corps . . . So sad. Signor Lomax was a man much loved.'

But not, perhaps, much known; certainly not by Signor Caramelli, who got his name wrong several times in the conversation that followed.

Nor, perhaps, by Herr Stückenmeier, who came in afterwards.

'So sorry,' he said. 'Deepest regrets. That such a thing should happen to so popular a figure as Mr . . . Mr . . . Lamberg? . . . comes as a shock to all of us.'

It was with some relief that Seymour heard an English voice in the office outside.

Its owner announced himself.

'Barton,' he said, holding out his hand. 'I'm the Peninsular man here. Sorry to hear about Lomax. I suppose that goes for all of us, although most of us didn't know him very well. He never had much to do with the Club.'

'Club?'

'The English Club. For people who work here. Only English, of course. Nothing against the Triestians, it's just that if you're with them all day, sometimes you want to get away.'

'But you say that Lomax . . .?'

'Wasn't like that.' Barton seemed puzzled. 'Spent all his time in the piazza. With Italians! Could never understand that. The man who was here before him – Shockley, his name was – was in the Club all the time.'

'Well, I suppose it take all sorts –'

'Yes. I know. But a consul ought not to be spending all his time with locals. He ought to be a bit detached. That's why it's useful to have a place like the Club. You can get away from everybody, be with your own. I daresay you'll find that.'

'Actually, I'm only here temporarily –'

'Just standing in? Well, at least they've got someone here

quickly. And that's important in a place like Trieste, where there are a lot of business interests. Look, you're very welcome to make use of the Club while you're here. Just sign yourself in. I'll look after the sponsoring.'

'Thank you. That's very kind of you.'

'Not at all.'

Barton held out his hand.

'I've got to push off, I'm afraid. Trouble at the docks again. Sorry about Lomax. Funny bloke. Can't say I really got on with him. Could never make him out. All right at his job, I will say that. But you never knew where you were with him. Too much in with the locals. You began to wonder whose side he was on.'

When the stream had subsided, Koskash came in.

'Schneider wants to see you,' he said.

'Fine, show him in.'

'No, no. You go to him, he doesn't come to you.'

'Well, all right, if that's the way it is. Where do I go?'

'The police station.'

'Police station?'

'There's a special part. Behind the main building.'

'Well, all right. And I just ask for Schneider, do I? Will that be enough?'

'Oh, yes. That will be enough.'

'Look, who the hell is Schneider?'

Koskash considered for a moment.

'In Trieste,' he then said carefully, 'there are two sorts of police.'

'Yes, yes, someone else has told me that.'

'The ordinary sort – Kornbluth is one of those. And – well, a different sort. The special police. They deal mostly with political matters.'

'Well, I'm like that. Mostly.'

'You are?' Koskash looked at him evenly. 'Well, then, you and Schneider should get on.'

*   *   *

Inside the room a man was sitting at a desk. He wore a
general's uniform and had close-cropped hair and a scar -
a duelling scar? – on his cheek.

'Herr Seymour? From the British Consulate?'

He rose and shook hands.

'I was very sorry to hear – we were all very sorry to hear.
Please accept our profound regrets. You may assure London that we shall do everything we can to track down
those responsible.'

'Thank you.'

Schneider looked at him curiously.

'You are not, I think, a regular member of the Consulate?'

'No. It happened that I was on my way here when –
when the incident happened. I am a King's Messenger.'

'Ah, a King's Messenger?' He looked at Seymour's wrist
and smiled. 'So it's true, then,' he said, 'about the watches?
You people always wear two?'

'Not always,' said Seymour.

'And that one is always set at British time, the other at
Continental time?'

'When it is important.'

Schneider laughed.

'Do you know what that says? To me, at any rate. It says
that British time is different from Continental time. That
Britain is always out of step with Europe. That our interests are always, in the end, different.'

'Why should our interests be different?' asked Seymour.

'Well,' said Schneider – he seemed to be watching him,
'take this matter of your Mr Lomax.'

'Why should our interests be different there? The Austrian authorities are surely as anxious as we are to find out
what happened to him?'

'Yes, of course we have to find out. And if a crime has
been committed, it must be solved. We can agree about
that. But beyond that?'

'Beyond that?'

'There may, of course, be nothing beyond that. It may all
be very simple. He goes out for the night with one of his

51

drunken friends and gets knocked on the head down by the docks. The body is thrown in the water. A simple robbery: that is all. Anyway, London says, that is all there is to it and it ends there. But suppose Vienna says, well, no, we do not think that is all there is to it and we would like to know more. Well, then, you see, our interests may differ. British time is not the same as Vienna time.'

'Why shouldn't that be all there is to it?'

'May I ask,' said Schneider, 'if you knew Lomax? Personally, I mean?'

'No.'

'I did. And I found him . . . surprising. At first when you meet him you think he is insignificant. You think there is nothing there. The sort of man you can walk over. And at first, when you do business with him, you do walk over him. But then, just when you think it's all over and done with, up he pops again, with that slightly inane smile of his, polite, deferential – deferring, always deferring. Everyone else's opinion is always better than his. Even when he is a drunken layabout. He defers even to the port officials and they think: this is an easy touch. No problem here. So they try to trick him. And they think they've got away with it. But no, suddenly it is not so easy. There he is popping up again. And in the end it is they who give way. It is almost exasperating. You could say, perhaps, that he is just very good at his job . . .

'But lately I have been wondering about your Mr Lomax. So ignorable, so overlookable, and yet so good at representing his country's interests. I have been asking myself recently where those interests end. There have been things, you see . . .

'And then one day he disappears. Consuls do not disappear. Just like that. Now I begin to wonder very hard. Is there something I have missed in this most missable of men? Something to do, perhaps, with those interests beyond the usual interests? Is this, perhaps, a point at which British time becomes different from Viennese time? And then he is found dead. And then . . .' Schneider

52

paused. '. . . a King's Messenger comes.' He was suddenly looking at Seymour very sharply. 'A King's Messenger?'

Seymour had had his doubts about the King's Messenger bit right from the first. It was always tricky to work covertly and to work covertly abroad even more tricky; especially when it was in a field completely new to you, as foreign, in all senses, as the diplomatic world. He had been able to see the argument for doing so in this case, however, and had allowed himself to be persuaded. What he had been more worried by, at the time, had been the difficulty of explaining it to his family.

He had had enough difficulty, with their history of dissent from government in their original native lands and the normal immigrant suspicion of authority in their new land, in getting them to accept his original decision to become a policeman. Now this!

It was his grandfather, surprisingly, who had recovered first. Although fiercely anti-royalist, he was disposed to make exceptions for the country of his adoption and found a perverse satisfaction in thinking now that his family had made it in England to the extent of his grandson becoming one of the King's courtiers, that, at last, one of his family promised to be on the inside of the power game. How wrong, thought Seymour, he was!

Seymour's mother, who thought that to take on any post with a title was to stick your neck out, remained doubtful, and his sister, who was probably the only one with an idea of what a King's Messenger actually was, was quietly dismissive.

His father stayed, as usual, silent. If his son was going to start travelling at the government's expense, why couldn't he go to the Baltic, where he might be able to do a useful bit of timber business on the side?

Now suddenly, almost as soon as he had got out to Trieste, to find himself under pressure on the covert side, was disconcerting. Schneider was sharp, no question about that. But what was he on about? He seemed to be hinting that Lomax might have played some other role in addition to that of consul. Just fancy, or was there something in it? Seymour was beginning to wonder if his briefing at the Foreign Office in London had been as full as it might have been.

He answered, however, neutrally.

'King's Messenger, yes. I was on my way here when it happened. Pure accident, of course.'

'Of course. I just hope that another accident doesn't happen.'

The artists, too, had heard the news and were in sombre mood at their table when he passed it that evening.

'Your friend,' said Lorenzo sorrowfully.

'Our friend,' said Luigi. 'How can such things happen?'

They invited him to join them but, slightly mindful of Barton's words, Seymour politely declined. They did not press him, thinking that he might wish to be alone this evening. He found a table by himself further on down towards the sea front.

Later on, however, he looked up to see Maddalena standing beside him.

'I am sorry,' she said.

He half rose and offered the chair opposite him. She hesitated for a moment and then sat down.

'I will not stay,' she said. 'You wish to be alone. I know.'

'There's a lot to think about,' said Seymour.

'Yes. He was your friend. I understand.'

Seymour nodded, feeling rather fraudulent, however.

'You will wish to find out who did it,' said Maddalena suddenly.

'Well . . .' said Seymour, startled.

Maddalena put her hand on his arm.

'I understand. We are like that, too.'

'Like . . .?'

'Had he no family?'

'Not much of one. Just an aunt. And an uncle. They had looked after him, I think, when he was a child.'

Maddalena nodded.

'They would be old, then, and not able to take it on themselves.'

'Take it on themselves?'

'The obligation. I understand. And so you, as a friend, must take it on.'

'Take it on?'

'It is a question of honour. You need say no more. I understand.'

'Just a minute –'

Maddalena got up from the table.

'I will leave you,' she said. 'You wish to be alone. I just wanted you to know that Lomax was my friend too. Perhaps more than a friend. And I wish to stand beside you. It is my obligation, too. We will work together.'

'Yes, well, thank you, but –'

But Maddalena had already gone.

Later, on his way back to the hotel, he passed the artists again, and again they invited him to join them. Feeling that it would be churlish to refuse, he sat down.

'Just a coffee, though,' he stipulated.

'You are welcome,' said Alfredo.

'Doubly welcome,' said Lorenzo.

'James has been arrested,' said Luigi.

'And we want you to get him out,' said Maddalena.

'Well, look, I don't know that I –'

'Lomax would have done. He was always going down to the police station. Not just for James but for any of us.'

'It is, actually, *easier* in the case of James than it would be for us,' said Alfredo, 'because James is a British national.'

'Look, I am just a Messenger.'

'A *King's* Messenger,' said Maddalena with emphasis.

'That doesn't mean a thing. It's a very lowly position, really.'

'Ah, but they won't know that.'

'I have no official standing.'

'Well, I think it's very unkind of you,' said Maddalena. 'James is your friend, isn't he?'

'No! I've never met him.'

'But he's our friend. Isn't that the same thing?'

'Well, of course, it does make a difference, but – look, what's he supposed to have done?'

'Drunk and disorderly, I expect,' said Alfredo.

'There!' said Maddalena. 'It's unjust! Everyone's drunk in Trieste.'

'But not always disorderly, Maddalena,' said Lorenzo judiciously. 'They don't always fight.'

'Well, James doesn't always fight. Not always.'

'Not when he's completely unconscious, no.'

'It's usually only when they want to throw him out because he hasn't paid.'

'There you are,' said Maddalena. 'Easy! Lomax would have settled it in no time.'

'Why don't *you* go down?' said Seymour.

'They won't take any notice of us.'

'They won't take any notice of *me*.'

'Yes, they will. You're an official. They take notice of officials.'

'They *only* take notice of officials,' said Lorenzo.

'Especially foreign officials,' said Luigi persuasively.

'Look, I'm *not* an official. I'm just a . . .'

In the end Seymour said that he was going to see Kornbluth the next day and that he *might*, he just might, mention it in passing.

Kornbluth was pleased.

'I think we're getting somewhere,' he said. 'The ticket! It

was as I supposed. It's one of the Edison's. And one of the new ones. Not only that!'

He paused triumphantly.

'Something else!'

'Something even better. One of our experts worked on it with the Edison staff and was able to establish that it was a ticket for . . .' He paused again. '. . . the performance on the night that he disappeared!'

'That's fantastic!'

'Pretty good, yes? I don't always hold with experts. They're sometimes a pain in the ass, they think they know it all, but I will say this, Ludwigsen really knows his onions. He's pretty confident about it. It was for the ten o'clock performance. Lomax must have gone there straight from the Piazza Grande. It is the lead we were looking for. And already we have found out something else.'

'You have?'

'We have.' Kornbluth paused impressively. 'He did not go alone.'

'Ah!'

'He was seen with someone. A man. Apparently they often go together. That's how they were spotted. They go so often that the usher has got to know them. He's positive that they were there that night.'

'Well, that *is* helpful.'

'We've got the man,' said Kornbluth.

'Already?'

'We sometimes move quite quickly,' said Kornbluth with pride.

'Clearly! And have you questioned him yet?'

'He admits he was there. That night. And with Lomax.'

'Well, that's tremendous. Congratulations!'

'Thank you.'

Kornbluth bowed acknowledgement.

'He says it was a standing arrangement. They would usually go to a cinema, one or other of them, every week.

57

That night it was the Edison. There was a picture that they particularly wanted to see.'

'What about afterwards? After they left the cinema?'

'He says that he went home. His wife confirms that. Of course, she would. But the concierge does, too. That, too, means little. And then, of course, there is the question of whether it was straight home. Well, we are looking into that.'

'And Lomax?'

'He says he doesn't know. He assumes he went home. When he left, he was standing there as if he was about to. But that, too, we can check.'

He clapped Seymour on the back.

'Things to do, yes? But at least we're starting to get somewhere.'

'It's excellent!'

'We are not always so bad,' said Kornbluth modestly.

'What about the other man?' asked Seymour. 'Do you know anything about him?'

'Oh, yes. We are old friends. We have had an eye on him for some time. He is a *professore* in the languages school here. He teaches English.'

'English?'

'He is English. That is, perhaps, how your Mr Lomax came to know him.' Kornbluth frowned. 'But he is not a good man for a consul to know. He is disreputable.'

Another one! Seymour's heart sank.

'Always he is in trouble. Drinking. Fighting.'

'Fighting?' said Seymour.

'Always.'

'His name is not James, by any chance?'

'James? No, I do not think so. It is Juice. Ah, no, I have it. It *is* James. A Mr James Juice.'

Chapter Five

Somewhat to his surprise, Seymour found himself after all walking out of the police station with him. There were no grounds on which to hold him and Kornbluth had for the moment finished his questioning. He was a tall, lanky, dishevelled Irishman who looked around at everything and everyone, including Seymour, with bloodshot, suspicious eyes.

'There's somebody to see you,' Kornbluth had announced cheerfully when they entered the cell.

'Why should I see him?'

'He's from the Consulate.'

'What's that to do with me?'

'You're English, aren't you?'

'No.'

'He's Irish,' said Seymour, picking up the accent.

The man looked at him as if he was seeing him for the first time.

Kornbluth shrugged.

'Anyway, you can go,' he said. 'For the time being.'

He shambled out. Kornbluth and Seymour exchanged glances, and shrugs.

Seymour followed him out and found him standing unsteadily on the pavement.

'Can you manage? Do you want me to see you home?'

'Home?' said James doubtfully. 'No, I need a drink. The piazza.'

They went there together.

'Who are you?' he said, after a moment.

Seymour decided he wouldn't say 'a friend of Lomax's' this time because this man actually was a friend of Lomax's.

'I'm from the Consulate,' he said.

'A replacement? Already?'

'No. I'm a King's Messenger. Just passing through.'

The Irishman nodded.

'Lomax,' he said: 'Kornbluth said they'd found him.'

'Yes, that's right.'

They walked on in silence.

After a while, Seymour said: 'You knew him well?'

'I used to see him nearly every day in the piazza. He helped me a lot over the cinema, too.'

'Cinema?'

'Business.'

'You were in business together?'

'No, no. He just helped me. When I needed advice.'

'And it was to do with a cinema?'

'Yes.' His attention seemed to waver. Then he pulled himself together. 'Yes, business,' he said. 'I'm a business-man.' He considered for a moment, then frowned. 'No, that's not right,' he said. 'I *would* have been a business-man.' He thought some more. 'But that's not right, either. I *was* a businessman.'

He looked at Seymour.

'What is a businessman?' he demanded.

'Well –'

'A man who does business. And did not I do business? Ergo . . .'

'I thought,' said Seymour cautiously, 'that you were a *professore*?'

'That, too,' said James grandly. 'What are these things anyway? Stops on the way to identity. Bus stops,' he said, with satisfaction. 'Businessmen are bus stops. That seems right. I, too, was a bus stop.'

'Ye-e-s?'

'For a while. Briefly. The imagination can enter into anything. Even a bus stop.'

60

'Ye-e-s? Yes, I'm sure. And this was to do with . . . the cinema, was it?'

'Beacons. I think of them as beacons. Beacons of light in a dark, backward world. Marinetti says that they are outposts of the future. All art, he says, is an outpost. Well, that is true, I think. But is it an outpost of the future? Is not art outside time? Not if it is a cinema. The cinema is definitely in time. Marinetti is right there.'

James stopped in the middle of the road and spread his arms.

'What I wished to do,' he said, 'was to light beacons in my benighted land. I lit one, I almost lit two. And then the money ran out.'

'Sorry?'

'Cinemas. "Here in Trieste," I said, "there are twenty-one cinemas. How many are there in Dublin? One. If O'Riley's is still going." That is what I said to Machnich. "There is an opportunity," I said. That is the thing about the imagination. It sees possibilities. That is why artists should be businessmen. And businessmen, artists. Only I did not say that last bit to Machnich. He might not have understood.'

'You were going to open cinemas in Dublin?'

'Going to? I did open them. One, anyway. It was very successful. I was going to open another when the bastard pulled the rug out from under me. "Too big a risk," he said. "Think of the return!" I said. "What return?" he said. "The one that will come in the future," I said. "It's not your money," he said. "How much have you put in?" "I've put in my talent," I said. It was an unequal bargain, but he didn't see it like that.'

'And Lomax helped in this enterprise?'

'Smoothed the way. The technicalities. Customs, Board of Trade, that sort of thing. It gave Machnich confidence, I think, to have Lomax advising. These things were important to him.'

'Did Lomax put in any money of his own?'

'Oh, dear, no! Machnich was the one with the money. He runs a big carpet shop. And the Edison, too. And one or two others. He wanted to run more. But Trieste is already

61

full of them. "Raise your eyes," I said. "Look outwards. Look to Ireland." I thought I had persuaded him. But in the end he hadn't the imagination. The money, but not the imagination.'

From the fact that Kornbluth had released James so readily, Seymour guessed that he didn't really suspect him of involvement in Lomax's death. He had probably worked out the kind of man James was. Seymour put him down as a batty professor who was too fond of his drink. He was involved only to the extent that he happened to be the person who had gone to the cinema with Lomax. There was nothing more sinister in it than that.

However, Kornbluth was right. They had learned something. They knew now that Lomax had gone to the Edison that night and that what had happened to him had happened after he came out. Seymour felt again the frustration of having to operate covertly. What he would have liked to do was question everyone in the vicinity and establish if anyone had seen Lomax at that point. But that was exactly what he couldn't do. He would have to leave that to Kornbluth.

When they got back to the piazza the artists were all sitting there at the table. They jumped up when they saw James and embraced him.

'There! You see?' said Maddalena, placing her hand intimately over Seymour's. 'It was easy.'

'What was it for this time, James?' asked Lorenzo.

James looked bewildered.

'I don't know,' he said. 'Going to the cinema, I think.'

'But, James –'

'Arresting people for going to the cinema?' cried Alfredo, firing up. 'Where will it end?'

'I don't think –' began Seymour.

His voice was drowned in the general protestation.

'They are standing out against the Future,' shouted Marinetti.

There was a new face at the table. It belonged to a middle-aged man with tobacco-stained fingers, whom they referred to as Ettore. During a lull in the conversation Seymour asked if he was an artist too. Alas, no, he said: his talents lay in other directions. He worked in the family varnishing business. He would soon, he said, be going to England to set up a factory there. In preparation for this he was taking, God help him, thought Seymour, lessons in English from James. A little later he shook hands all round and left.

After he had gone Alfredo said that although he was not an artist he understood about artists. He was a writer and had written several novels. None of them had got anywhere and he had given up writing; but recently he seemed to have started again.

Perhaps it was the effect of Lomax's death that they drank heavily. Seymour reckoned himself to have a good head for alcohol but he found it hard to keep level. He wondered uneasily who was going to pay and if he should. Could he put it down to expenses? Almost certainly not, he thought.

When it came to it, they all insisted that he was their guest and that there could be no question of his paying; but as they turned out their pockets it looked rather as if they were going to be his. In fact, however, Ettore had already paid.

As he was going away across the piazza he saw a newspaper seller standing there with his newspapers spread out on the ground before him. He was holding up a newspaper and shouting: 'Bosnia crisis! The latest.'

Crisis? What crisis? Almost: Bosnia? What Bosnia?

Seymour could never resist a headline. He went across to the man and bought one of his papers.

As far as he could see, there was no mention of Bosnia in it.

'Hey, what was all that about a crisis?' he complained to the newspaper seller.

'It's still there.'

'It doesn't say anything about a crisis here!'

'It doesn't need to. I'm saying it. It's still on. That's the point. I don't want people to forget about it.'

'Yes, but the newspaper isn't saying anything about it!'

'It bloody well ought to be. That's why I'm saying it.'

'Yes, well, thanks. Don't you think you should leave editorial comment to the editors?'

'No. They're all bloody Austrian. You won't find a word about this now that it's happened. They want to keep it quiet.'

'Look, *what's* happened? What crisis is this, anyway?'

'The annexation.'

'What annexation?'

'Christ, where have you come from?'

'London.'

'Isn't it in all the papers there?'

'No.'

'Well, it bloody ought to be. It's a disgrace. More than a disgrace, it's a conspiracy. All the Great Powers hanging together. And letting Austria hang Bosnia.'

'Just tell me.'

'You don't know? Really? Christ, you're an ignorant bugger.'

'Tell me.'

'Well, you know that a couple of years ago Austria annexed Bosnia. No? You really don't?'

'It had escaped me.'

'What hope is there for the working class when the privileged classes are so bloody ignorant! Well, it did. Just like that. They thought no one would notice. And if you're anything to go by, they were dead right. All right, you're an ignorant Britisher. But you'd have thought *someone* would have noticed and said: "Hey, you can't do that!" But they're all in it together, the Great Powers.'

'Yes, well, no doubt. But it's all over, isn't it? You said it was two years ago?'

'It's not all over. It's never going to be all over. It's going to blow up.'

64

'Yes, well, maybe.'

'It'll blow up. And blow your world apart.'

'Yes, yes.'

'How do you think the Bosnians feel about it? How do you think *we* feel about it?'

'We? What's it got to do with Trieste?'

'I'm speaking as a Serb.'

'All right, speaking as a Serb: what's it got to do with Serbia?'

'Well, Bosnia's bloody ours, isn't it? Or it ought to be. It's been part of Serbia for a thousand years. Or it should have been. And do you think we're going to let them get away with this? Not a chance!'

Seymour went to Lomax's apartment and began making a list of his effects. He was sitting at the small table when Maddalena came in.

'The concierge let me in.' She looked at Seymour. 'But I have a key, yes.'

'Why have you come here?' asked Seymour.

'To see if I could find anything here that would help us.'

'Help us to do what?'

'Find out who killed him.'

Seymour sighed.

'Hadn't you better leave that to the police?'

'Are *you* leaving it to the police?' she said.

'No,' he said, after a moment.

'Well, I'm not, either.'

'What were you hoping to find?' he said.

'Names.'

'There aren't any. I've looked.'

'Do you mind if I look? I know the place better than you.'

'Go ahead.'

Some time later she came back.

'You're right,' she said. 'There aren't any.'

'He never put anything on paper.'

'No,' she said.

'Were you looking for any names in particular?'

65

She was silent for a little while. Then she said: 'Lomax helped a lot of people. I thought that one time it might have gone wrong.'

'Do you have any particular reason for thinking that?'

She was silent again. She seemed to be turning something over in her mind. At last she said:

'It seems silly. Trivial. It is probably nothing. But since – since it happened, since Lomax died, I have been thinking, thinking all the time. How could it have happened? How could anyone have done that to – well, a person like him? I have thought over everything, the people he knew, the things he did. But he never did a bad thing. I am sure he would never do a bad thing. So why would anyone want to kill him? I have thought and thought. And the conclusion I have come to is that it must be because of one of the good things he did. Perhaps it went wrong, or perhaps they wanted more. More than he was prepared to give.

'Because he was quite strong, really. Stronger than you thought. I know he didn't seem like that. Not when you first met him. When he first joined us in the piazza – Alfredo, I think it was, or perhaps Ettore, who brought him – we thought, what a funny little man! I mean, he didn't fit in at all. He knew nothing about art, that was obvious, or about artists. He wasn't interested in any of the things we were interested in. But he kept on coming. We couldn't think why he bothered. He never used to say anything. He just sat there smiling, like a puppy wagging its tail. And that's how we treated him, like a little dog, who had for some reason attached itself to us.

'He was so grateful to be stroked. And then I saw that he was especially grateful to be stroked by me. I quite enjoyed that, any woman does, giving the occasional stroke from time to time and watching a man wag his tail. It become obvious. "You have made a conquest there, Maddalena," the others said. I wasn't very flattered. "Well, I'm not surprised," I said, "A man like that!" He seemed so silly, you know, with that inane smile and his moustache, and those dog-like eyes. But gradually he grew on me. It is nice to be worshipped.'

'And so you came to have the key to his apartment,' said Seymour.

'Yes. And at one time I used to come here often. Then, not so much. Only when I needed to. A woman on her own sometimes needs someone to go to. The others – Alfredo and Luigi and Lorenzo – are all right, but they are artists. They see me as a model and not always as a person. But sometimes you feel the need to be seen as a person. Well, when it was like that, I would go to Lomax.

'But it wasn't just me. We all turned to him when we were in difficulties, when there was some business problem or trouble with the authorities. Whenever James got put in prison, for example. And he always knew what to do. He would always be able to sort it out. In the Austrian Empire it is always difficult if you come up against the officials. They ride rough-shod over you, especially if you are just an ordinary person. But the officials could never fob Lomax off or browbeat him or override him. That is what I meant when I said that he was so strong.

'And he always used it for others. I have been thinking about him a lot since he died and that is what I have come to see, and what is so wonderful.'

She had begun to cry a little.

'And that is why I feel so angry. It is so – so unjust. That he should die like this. God is unjust and must not be allowed to get away with it. I will not let that happen. I, Maddalena, will not let that happen,' she said, fiercely, through her tears.

'I am sorry. You obviously knew him much better than I did and cared for him deeply –'

'No!'

'No?'

'No. I cared for him shallowly, too shallowly. It has been over for some time. It is nice to be worshipped but to be up on a pedestal for too long is boring. And wrong, anyway. It is not what I want from a man. It was time to move away. Time, too, for him to move away. I think he had begun to realize that for himself. I was part, you see, of his first days in Trieste, and they were over.

67

'When he first came to Trieste, something happened to him. There was a great opening up – art, sunshine, the Mediterranean way of life, it all hit him together. All his life up till then he had been contained, controlled. Now, suddenly, he felt free. Things became possible that had not seemed possible before. Love, perhaps. Me.

'He found it all in me, you see. Or thought he did. Love, art, release, freedom – everything. Of course, it was not there. I am much less than that. But perhaps for him, for a while, it was there.

'For a while. But then, you see, I think he began to grow. This opening up did not stop there. He looked at things he had not noticed before, things he had never previously questioned. Things about society. About people. Perhaps he thought: I am free, why cannot they be free?

'He began to look outwards, to involve himself more with other people. He began to help them. But, you know, in Trieste people are not just people, they are always part of something else. I don't think he realized that. I don't think he realized that though you may begin with helping people as individuals, you are soon, in Trieste, drawn on to helping other things. And that, I think, is what may have happened to him. He was drawn on and then it went wrong.

'You asked me if I had any particular reason for thinking that. Yes, I do. Once – I remember when it was. There was a big reception at the Casa Revoltella and he asked me if I would come with him. Well, I did not want to go very much, it is not my kind of thing, pompous people, stiff uniforms – no, no. But he said: "Oh, do come, Maddalena! If I don't have someone real to talk to, I shall go crazy! And there will be lots of colour and beautiful things and you can point them out to me."

'Well, I agreed. But then, on the day before it was going to happen, he came to me and said: "No, no, I can't go. It would not be right. Someone else has asked me to take them, and I don't want to. It would not be right." "If you're bothered about me, you needn't be," I said. "I'm quite happy not to go. Why don't you take this other person?" "No," he said. "It would be better for me not to go at all. That would make it clear." Well, I tried to persuade him, but he would not have it, and I didn't try too hard. It was not important to me. But afterwards I thought about it and I couldn't understand it. Who was this other person? Why didn't he want to go with them? And why was it so important? I did not find answers, but now the questions come back to me.'

She shrugged.

'It may be nothing,' she said. 'Now when I tell it, it seems trivial. But it was a moment when I felt there was a side to Lomax, a part of his life, that I did not know. And that surprised me, for I felt that I knew everything about him. And now, after thinking about Lomax and searching and searching, trying to find what could have led to this, this is all I can think of. It is trivial, I know, perhaps silly, but it is all that I can come up with.'

'And so, when you came back here to look for names, this was the name you were looking for?'

She nodded.

'Do you think it might have been an Italian name?'

'I hope not,' she said.

The Mediterranean evening set in early and it was dark by the time Seymour got back to the Consulate. There was a light on. Koskash must still be there. Seymour hoped he had not stayed on because of him.

The front door was locked so he went round to the side door. It opened easily and he stepped in.

Koskash was at his desk. There were two men standing in front of him. They had their backs turned to the door and were blocking Koskash's view so that for a moment none of them knew that Seymour had come in.

'I can't do it,' Koskash was saying. 'Not now.'

'He needs them tonight,' one of the men insisted.

'I'm only half-way through doing them and I've got to go out.'

'He needs them. Tonight.'

Koskash looked up and saw Seymour.

'All right,' he said reluctantly. 'I'll see what I can do. Tell him to come later. Not too much later. Between nine and nine thirty. And if he's not here by nine thirty, it will be too bad, because I've got to go out.'

He ushered the men out.

'Seamen!' he said feelingly when he got back. 'They just don't understand. It's always got to be done immediately. They can't see that things take time.'

'They're lucky to catch you at this hour.'

'They wouldn't normally. It's just that my wife and I are going out later this evening and this is a good place for her to pick me up.'

Seymour went on into the inner room. It was too early to go to the cinema or to have a meal and Lomax's office, bare though it was, was more congenial than his hotel room.

He sat down at the desk and began to copy out the list of Lomax's effects. It would be needed back in London by whoever was winding up Lomax's estate.

Through the half-open door he could see Koskash working on assiduously. He saw him look at his watch.

'Nine thirty,' he said, catching Seymour's eye, 'and he's not come. Seamen!'

There was a knock on the side door.

'Ah!'

It was his wife, however. She was younger than Koskash and distinctly Slav in looks. She stopped when she saw Seymour, as if surprised, and then came forward, smiling.

'Koskash had told me about you,' she said. She called him Koskash. 'I hope you will enjoy your stay, even though it will obviously be a short one. And comes at such a sad time.'

They chatted for a while and then she looked at her husband.

'Oughtn't we to go?'

Koskash had tidied his papers up but was hesitating by his desk.

'There's someone coming,' he said.

70

'At twenty to *ten*? Look, if we don't leave soon, the meeting will have started.'

'It's – it's for papers,' said Koskash.

'Oh! Oh, well, in that case –'

'I'll be here for a bit longer,' said Seymour.

Koskash looked at his wife.

'That would be very kind,' she said, smiling. 'Are you sure you don't mind?'

'Not at all.'

'Don't hang around for him,' said Koskash. 'Leave when you want to and if he's not come, well, too bad.'

He and his wife went off arm in arm.

Seymour went back to his desk. It didn't take him long to finish his copying. Lomax hadn't had many effects.

It was getting towards ten now. If he wanted to get to the cinema in time for the evening performance, he would have to leave now. The man had probably decided not to come.

He put the papers he had been working on in the empty drawer of Lomax's desk, together with the envelope that Koskash had given him. Then he went out into the main office. Koskash had given him a key to the side door. He opened the door and went out.

As he stepped outside, he almost collided with a man about to come in. The man fell back with a surprised gasp.

'Signor Lomax?' he said hesitantly.

'No. Seymour. Have you come for something?'

'*Si. Si.*'

Seymour took him in. He was a young man in his twenties, wearing spectacles and in a cheap, dark suit. He brought his heels together and gave a little bow. Then he looked at Seymour uncertainly.

'I was expecting Koskash,' he said.

'He's just gone.'

'I am sorry, I am late. They said to be here before nine thirty but I took a wrong turning. I do not know Trieste.'

Reassured by the reference to the deadline Koskash had

71

appointed, Seymour went back into his room and fetched the envelope.

'Was this what you were wanting?'

The man looked in the envelope and nodded. He seemed relieved.

'Please will you thank Mr Koskash for me,' he said.

He spoke in Italian but was not Italian. Nor was he English. This troubled Seymour but for the moment he couldn't think why.

The man clicked his heels and bowed again, and Seymour let him out.

All day he had been listening to the voices around him: the women haggling in the markets, the men unloading the boats, the newspaper seller in the piazza, the barely comprehensible old woman behind her pile of melons; the little groups of men standing talking in the piazzas – they seemed to stand there all day; the housewives sitting in their doorway to catch a breath of air, calling back over their shoulder from time to time to someone inside, an elderly mother who would occasionally show herself, or a young daughter who would emerge indignant and passionate, holding an even younger child by the hand; the policemen at the police station with their Austrian *bittes* and the waiters in the Piazza Grande with their Italian *pregos*. All day he had been taking them in and now, sitting in the Edison, at the time that Lomax had sat there, waiting for the picture to begin, the picture that Lomax had waited for with James, he was listening to them still.

Seymour had an unusual ear for language. It was that that had brought him here, had made him what he was. Growing up in the East End and hearing its various languages he had sometimes mimicked them when he had gone home. Old Appelmann, visiting once, had noticed his facility and encouraged it. Occasionally he took Seymour with him when he was doing his work as the local interpreter, and had talked about the language after. Old Appelmann had once been a teacher and could not resist teaching now. Gradually, with his help, Seymour had acquired the languages of the East End.

Much of Appelmann's work had been for the police and in that way they had got to know Seymour too. That had led first to his becoming Appelmann's paid assistant and then to his joining the police force itself.

At first he had not liked the police and had thought about leaving. But acute superiors had spotted his talent, which was not confined to languages, and encouraged him to make use of it. In time he had settled and things suddenly became easier when, unusually for an ordinary constable, he had been transferred to the Special Branch. They had used him a lot in the East End, where so many languages were spoken.

Trieste, from that point of view, was a delight. It was like the East End only more so. It was Europe in miniature, Europiccola, as James had once said fondly, Europe with all its languages brought together in a small space.

Now, in the cinema, his ear trailed, as it were, lovingly over them; but all the time at the back of his mind he was hearing again the voice of the man who had come to the Consulate late to pick up his 'papers'. Something about it continued to niggle at him.

A piano at the front of the cinema started to play. The show was about to begin. It was the picture that Lomax had seen on the night he died. *Aladdin and the Magic Lamp.* Seymour felt an anticipating thrill of excitement. This, at any rate, should be a treat.

When Seymour came out of the cinema he found his path obstructed by a line of men carrying placards. In the darkness he couldn't quite see what the placards said. The men didn't really attempt to block him. They parted and let everyone through.

'Socialists!' said a man beside Seymour, contemptuously.

Chapter Six

In most parts of the East End uniformed policemen always went in twos. Seymour was usually not in uniform and, besides, knew the East End and was known in it, so he hadn't normally bothered to. Nevertheless, he always, and especially after dark, walked carefully. He had developed a sense which told him when he was being followed.

It was telling him now. He stopped outside a shop and looked in, as if he was examining the strings of brightly coloured and variously shaped pasta, and glanced back along the street. A man in a trilby hat was hovering outside a taverna. He seemed to make up his mind and went in. Further along the street two men were talking unhurriedly. An ox-cart came down the street and stopped outside the taverna. The driver and his mate got down and began to unload the barrels.

Seymour walked on. If it hadn't been for this he would have enjoyed the freshness of the morning, with its smells of baking and of coffee, the fresh smell of the water the shopkeepers were sprinkling on the dust they had just swept out of their shops, the freshness of the sea breeze creeping up into the tired, stale alleys.

After a while, as the feeling persisted, he turned aside into a small piazza where there was an open-air market. Fish gleamed on stalls, crabs hung from hooks, sea spiders glistened in shells. Seymour walked through the vegetable stalls loaded with aubergines and tomatoes and peppers of all colours, green, red and yellow, and then out on the other side to where melons were piled on the ground in mountains and where a mother was washing a small child's face, not in water, because the pump was on the other side of the market, but in melon juice.

He doubled round, turned up a side street, and came out on to the road he had originally been on. He did not step out on to it, however, but hung back in the shadow.

A little later he saw the man in the trilby hat come quickly out of the market and look up and down the street. He spotted Seymour and walked, seemingly casually, across the street to the other side and studied the contents of the window of a gentlemen's outfitter.

Seymour continued to be conscious of his presence behind. He never came close, however, so Seymour knew that this was a different kind of follower from the ones you got in the East End.

When he arrived at the Consulate Koskash handed him a large envelope from Kornbluth. It contained the preliminary medical findings on the body. He did not at once have time to read it, however, as two more people came to express formal condolence. They came from other consulates, of which there were, not surprisingly, a great many in Trieste. Seymour had been hoping, following the conversation with Maddalena yesterday, that someone else might come forward. Lomax had obviously had acquaintances from outside the diplomatic community. Where were they?

By the time he had got through the consular condolences it was late in the morning and the heat was building up. He decided to get away from the Consulate before anyone else came. He wanted to read in peace the material Kornbluth had sent him.

Koskash, ever polite, came with him to the door. Across the road, leaning apparently casually against a wall, was the man in the trilby.

Koskash laughed.

'So you, too, have been honoured! You know what they

say here? They say that in Trieste the sun is so bright that everyone has a shadow.'

So that was the kind of follower it was. Seymour was quite taken aback. Why should the authorities be watching *him*? The thought came into his mind that perhaps, having mislaid Lomax, they did not wish to mislay him. But that seemed unlikely. From what Koskash had said, it was almost a matter of routine, the style of the place. But what sort of place was it where everyone had a shadow?

He found himself near the Canal Grande and on an impulse turned in towards it and walked along beside the boats to the café where he and Kornbluth had sat the other day.

There were people already at the tables, clerks from the big offices looking down on the canal having their mid-morning coffee, storemen already three-quarters of their way through the day sitting down with the captains of the boats, discussing cargoes. In the boats themselves men were working hard on the loading and unloading. This was the time, before the sun got too high, to do the heavy work.

At the end of the canal the women were sitting again on the steps of the church stitching. Occasionally one of them would take her work down some steps on one side of the church. After a while, he thought he had worked it out. There was probably a basement workshop there. The women working there would rather do their stitching out-side on the steps.

As he watched, a small procession came out of one of the side streets and stopped in front of the church. It consisted mostly of women. Two held a banner, others gave out leaflets. One woman stood up beside the banner and began to address the women on the steps.

A man came up from the basement and shouted at the speaker, who took no notice. The man hurried away and the speaker went on speaking. The women on the steps listened quietly, no longer chattering.

Suddenly the man appeared once more, this time with a group of policemen. They barged at once into the procession, scattering people, banner and leaflets. Some women fell on to the steps. They picked themselves up, retrieved their leaflets and the banner and regrouped further along the quay.

Unnecessarily heavy-handed policing, thought Seymour, with the critical eye of the professional. Why not just tell them to move on? The other way merely stored up trouble.

The re-formed procession came down the quay towards Seymour but just before it reached him it turned off. There were about a dozen women and one or two shabbily dressed men. One of the women seemed familiar to Seymour but he didn't see how this could be and thought he must have make a mistake.

The procession came closely enough, however, for him to be able to read the banner. It was a Socialist banner of some sort; the Socialist Workers Party of Trieste, he thought he read.

He felt a twinge of nostalgia. Demonstrations like this were a familiar feature of the East End. Many of the immigrant families had been obliged to leave their original countries because of their political views and they often brought their principles with them. There were all sorts of little radical groups in the East End. They usually were little; most people followed the immigrant strategy of keeping their heads down. But there were always some who wouldn't, who argued that what was right in Hungary or Poland or wherever was right in England, too.

Seymour's own sister was one of these. She was a Socialist, too, which was why she came now into his mind. Socialism was quite strong in Whitechapel, especially among the Jews and in the Jewish tailors' workshops which were common in the East End, workshops like the one at the end of the canal. She had started going to Socialist meetings when she was still at school and that had led on to other things, to fundraising bazaars, to taking part in demonstrations like this one and to standing on street corners distributing leaflets.

That was the bit that had got Seymour. He had no objection to Socialism as such. In the East End you rather took it for granted. It was the things that went with it.

When the children were small, Seymour's mother had had to go out to work, which meant that his sister had had to look after him. She had taken him to the meetings she attended, which were often in private houses. It was there that he had first met the various languages of the East End. When he had gone home he had mimicked them, and it was hearing him do this that had made Old Appelmann realize the boy's extraordinary ear.

Seymour hadn't minded that part. What he had minded was being obliged by his sister to stand embarrassingly on some cold shop corner accosting the passers-by.

He was remembering this, wryly, when it suddenly came into his mind where he had seen before the woman in the group who had seemed familiar. She was Koskash's wife.

There was nothing unexpected in the medical report. Lomax had died from a single heavy blow to the back of the head. The body had then been thrown into the water. Its condition was consistent with its having been in the sea for a week to ten days.

There was some ancillary bruising but that had probably come from contact with rocks after the body had been thrown in the sea. There were no wounds of a sort to indicate that Lomax had put up a struggle, that he had not been taken completely by surprise. This was a preliminary report: perhaps the final autopsy would reveal more. It was good of Kornbluth, however, to send it him.

He put the report down on the table. It didn't add much to what he already knew. What seemed clear was what had been clear without the report: Lomax must have been killed near the water. You wouldn't want to lug a body too far. That meant he must have walked down to the sea after leaving the Edison. Why had he done that? To freshen up after having been in the hot cinema, take a second, late *passeggiatta* as it were? Or for some other reason: to meet someone, perhaps. For what reason? Pleasure or business? But what business could Lomax have had, down by the docks, probably, so late at night?

The artists were in their usual spot. There seemed, however, to be an argument going on.

'Now!' he heard Marinetti's angry voice. 'Now he tells me!'

'Well, I'm sorry,' said a voice that was new to Seymour. It came from an upright, smart-looking man, new to the group, who didn't seem a bit sorry. A thin smile played on his lips. It was almost as if he was enjoying Marinetti's rage. 'Mr Machnich, however, has had second thoughts.'

'But he can't have second thoughts. Not as late as this! When it was all agreed. Look, it's happening on Saturday! Next Saturday!'

'It will have to happen somewhere else,' said the new man, still with his thin smile. 'That's all.'

'But, Jesus, I've arranged it. We'd agreed!'

'And now it's disagreed.'

'Machnich can't do this to me!'

'You'll just have to find another place.'

'There *isn't* another place. Not at such short notice. And not as suitable as the Politeama. Look, it's going to be big. There are going to be hundreds of people there. Only the Politeama will do.'

'Well, I'm sorry, but Mr Machnich has changed his mind.'

'Look, there's money in this. For him.'

'I doubt it,' said the new man, sceptically.

'Money. You tell him that. Money! That's the only thing that'll interest that bastard.'

The other artists joined in.

'Too true.'

'You can say that again!'

'This is *important*!' said Marinetti, his voice rising. 'I've got people coming from all over Europe.'

'Oh, yes,' said the new man, his voice oozing doubt.

'Yes!' roared Marinetti. 'You dumb-headed Bosnian! Can't you understand? We shall be reading our Manifesto. This is the birth of a new movement. A movement which will change art, and the world, for ever!'

'Art, is it? I don't think Mr Machnich is very interested in art.'

'Well, no, he wouldn't be. But he is interested in money. Tell him there's money in this.'

'Not as much as there is in wrestling.'

'Wrestling?'

'That's what he'll be putting on instead.'

'Wrestling!'

'Yes. Serbia versus Austria. The place will be packed.'

'Look, this was agreed months ago. He can't pull out now.'

'No?'

'Look. I could run perhaps to just a little more money.'

'No, you couldn't. You can't even run to what was agreed.'

'Why is he doing this?'

'Reason broke in. In the end.'

'You talked him out of it. You bastard!'

'He needs a little guidance occasionally.'

'He needs a little guidance about keeping his word. But he wouldn't be getting that from you, would he?'

The man began to get up.

'It's a waste of time talking,' he said. 'We've made up our minds.'

'You dumb idiot! You're turning down the chance of a lifetime!'

The man laughed.

'We're pulling out of a big flop. You'll never fill the Politeama. Not with what you're planning.'

'You're wrong, you're wrong. I've sent out invitations. And I've had replies. Dozens of them. Hundreds.'

'Oh, yes?'

'The Governor –'

'Well, I can tell you that he certainly won't be coming.'

'Oh, yes, he will.'

'I don't think so.'

'His wife is on the organizing committee.'

The man stopped.

'What?'

'On our committee. She's interested in art. Not like you, you philistine bastard.'

The man turned and came back.

'Are you having me on?'

'No, I'm not. You wait and see. Just wait till I tell her that Machnich says we must scrap the whole thing because he can't keep his word!'

'If you're lying to me –'

'Lying? To the man who has Machnich's ear? Would I do that? I'd sooner spit in it.'

'I shall check this –'

'Check all you like, you dumb idiot!'

The man hesitated.

'You're sure about this? Really sure?'

'As sure as I am that you're a stupid, ignorant –'

'The Governor?'

'And the consuls. And the Chamber of Commerce. Everybody. Everybody who's anybody.'

'If you're having me on –'

'The Governor. His wife has promised. And if it's the Governor, it's going to be everyone else, isn't it?'

The man hesitated.

'If you like,' said Marinetti, 'I'll go round and tell her now. I'm sorry, Frau Kruger, but Machnich says –'

'All right, all right. All right, you can have it. You can have the Politeama for the evening.'

'Thank you. It's so nice of you to keep your word. And surprising.'

'Shut up!' said the new man, wavering still. 'The Governor? You're sure?'

'And his wife,' said Marinetti, beaming.

'The consuls? The diplomatic riff-raff? They're the ones who matter. You're sure about them?'

'If the Governor is there, so will they be.'

He made up his mind, finally.

'All right then. Don't cock it up.'

'Shall I send Machnich an invitation?'

'Why not?' said the man, smiling his thin smile.

'What a bastard!' said Luigi.

'Who is he?' asked Seymour.

'His name is Rakic. He does things for Machnich.'

'He seems pretty confident that Machnich will agree to whatever he says.'

'I don't know why he should be. He hasn't been here five minutes.'

'And the sooner he goes away again, the better.'

'They say he was in the army.'

'Well, it certainly sounds like it. Let's have a drink. To take the taste out of our mouths. Giuseppi!'

Seymour was going to leave but they insisted that he have one too. Marinetti pulled up a chair. Seymour sat down next to him.

'What's this you're putting on?'

'Ah! My Evening. Well . . .' began Marinetti enthusiastically.

The others moved away. They had heard it, Seymour suspected, many times before.

'The first Futurist Evening!'

'Futurist?'

'That's what we call ourselves. The Futurists. Art must look forward. Not back.'

'Yes, yes, I'm sure.'

'Art . . .'

Seymour began to wish that he had moved away too.

Seymour went back to the Consulate. Koskash was, as he always seemed to be, bent over his desk. He laid his pen down.

'I would like,' said Seymour, 'to get a feel for the work of the Consulate. The kind of things Lomax did. The kind of things you do.'

'Certainly!' said Koskash enthusiastically. 'I'd be glad to show you –'

Seymour interrupted him hastily, fearing he was about to be exposed to another dose like Marinetti's.

'Something simple. Those papers you were working on the other night, for instance.'

'Well, they are hardly typical. That sort of thing comes up only every so often.'

'Never mind. They'll do for a start. Now what exactly were you doing?'

'Making out papers for seamen. Usually because they've lost them. Or had them stolen. That happens sometimes, usually when they've been to a brothel or a taverna.'

Seymour went through the process with him. It seemed a simple clerical matter, recorded meticulously in Koskash's careful handwriting.

'You keep a record, of course?'

'Oh, yes. We have to. So that we can check up if the need arises. There's a certain market in such papers.'

'And you keep the record . . .?'

'Over there. In the files.'

A little of this kind of thing went a long way and Seymour soon thanked Koskash, saying that he would come back for enlightenment on another process.

'The stationery inventory, perhaps?' said Koskash enthusiastically.

'Perhaps,' said Seymour, backing off.

*   *   *

When Koskash had finished work for the day, almost regretfully, it seemed, he went off. Seymour remained at his desk, writing his report. After Koskash had left, he went over to the files and found the folder containing the duplicates of the seamen's papers that Koskash had made out. There were, as Koskash had said, not many of them, but Seymour went back over several years, until a different Consul's name appeared in the records.

As Seymour left the Consulate, he sensed, rather than saw, the man in the trilby hat falling in behind him. Was this the way it was going to be every time he went out? If it was, he didn't like it. It made the place feel different, put a shadow over the sun. Why him? Why should he be singled out in this way?

And then Koskash's words came back to him. Of course. He wasn't being singled out. This was everybody. Perhaps not everybody, it couldn't be. But enough people for it to be taken for granted. It was a permanent feature of the place, part of the landscape, part of the Trieste way of life. Almost something in the air you breathed. It had been there, he realized, all the time, behind the sunshine and the sparkling sea, behind the wine and the waiters and the tables in the great piazza, behind the liners at anchor in the bay. It was just that at first he had not seen it.

It had been there, he realized, in the soldiers at the entrance of every official building, in the policemen at every public place where people gathered; There in the inspectors present in every market, however small, and anywhere where things were done.

There, in the uniforms everywhere, with their precise, pretty distinctions, the different sorts of epaulettes, the cocked hats for one grade of functionary, the flat caps for another, in the subtly differential braid and the tightly prescribed brims.

In the prescribed sheets of paper, the 'chancery double', on which every official transaction or application, however trivial, had to be written, and which was available in every office and shop; in the forms he had to fill in at the hotel and in the 'papers' he had to present on countless occasions.

The night before he had left, when he had been packing his suitcase, at one point he thought he had lost his papers.

'For God's sake!' his grandfather had cried in anguish. 'What are you doing? Papers are important to these bastards. If you don't have papers, they shut you up.'

'That was the Tsarist police, Grandfather,' his sister had murmured patiently.

'The Hapsburg police are no different, are they, Else?' He had appealed to Seymour's mother.

'The Hapsburg police are worse,' she said firmly.

'It's all right, I've got them,' Seymour had said, as his sister found them and threw them to him.

'Then you see you keep them!' thundered his grandfather. 'No papers, no person! That is how it is with the Hapsburgs. You remember that! It is not like England.'

'No, it is not!' echoed his mother.

Seymour had caught his sister's eye, in the complicit shrugging of shoulders that one generation had for another.

But now he suddenly thought that they might have been right. It wasn't just a toothless bureaucratic fuss about paper, it was a bureaucracy with an edge of steel.

It was part of that other thing that was there, almost in the air, of Trieste; there in the very buildings, in the heaviness and grandiosity of the architecture, in the height of the official rooms, and the width of the staircases and the thickness of the carpeting, in the marble finishing and the walnut woodwork.

There, most of all, in the portraits of the Emperor, in his peaked military cap and white tunic, displayed in every official building and almost in every room, in Schneider's office, for instance, and in Kornbluth's, but also in every tobacconist's shop and in every bar and hotel.

The day before, he had gone to the Maritime, the fine, classical building on the waterfront which housed the Ministry of Maritime Affairs. When Seymour had gone up the flight of stairs and into the marble-floored reception hall, what had struck him was the resemblance to the Foreign Office in London: the same confidence, the same air of superiority, the same grandiloquence.

It was, he realized now, the insignia of Empire. And it told of grip.

When he had entered the hall, Seymour, unused to such places, had stopped for a moment, slightly daunted. But then he had recovered. Was he not, after all, himself the representative of Empire? Even if not in proper person. He told himself wryly that his grandfather would have been proud of him.

Thinking about it now, however, he felt exactly what his grandfather would have felt: the tremor of rebellion.

That evening, going, as had now become as habitual to him as to the rest of the population of Trieste, to the Piazza Grande, he ran into Kornbluth, who invited him to join his table at the other end of the piazza.

As they walked down there, keeping time to the slow movement of the *passeggiatta*, Seymour thanked him for sending the medical report and asked him how he had been getting on that day.

'Badly,' said Kornbluth gloomily. 'I have not found a single person who saw him after he came out of the Edison. I have asked everyone in the piazza, down to the dog in the taverna.'

'I find –' began Seymour, and then shut up. He was not supposed to be a policeman.

Kornbluth did not seem to notice.

'Of course, we shall go round again tomorrow,' he said. 'And the next day. And probably the next. Spreading out.'

'Have you tried the docks?' said Seymour. 'He must have been killed near the sea.'

'We tried there first,' said Kornbluth.

'It might not have been the docks. Anywhere along the sea front. It could have been the bottom of the Piazza Grande.'

'Tried there,' said Kornbluth. 'And the Molo.'

'It's a big area.'

'And the red-light houses,' said Kornbluth. 'We've tried them too. You never know with these quiet people.'

He led Seymour to a table at which a plump, grey-haired lady was sitting. She smiled up at Seymour.

'We always sit here,' she said.

'My wife likes the music. And the dance, too, yes, Hilde?'

'And the dance, too,' said Hilde. 'Although preferably with someone lighter on his feet than my husband.'

'She likes the bandmaster, too,' said Kornbluth looking round roguishly. 'Is Lehar here this evening?'

'I hope so,' said his wife. 'Then at least we'll get some decent waltzes.'

'Hilde comes from Vienna,' said Kornbluth 'and thinks that only in Vienna do they know how to waltz.'

They were sitting at a table close to the bandstand and eventually a heavily pomaded man in military uniform appeared and brought the band to order. It began to play light, jolly music. Beneath the trees couples began to dance.

The band took a short break and then started to play again. This time it was a succession of waltzes. This was evidently what people had been waiting for because suddenly the space beneath the trees was full of couples dancing.

The lift of the music, the swirl of the dresses beneath the coloured lamps along the branches, the clink of the glasses and the laughter at the tables, the sea smell coming in and mixing with the scent of the flowers, drew more and more people to that end of the piazza.

Seymour was conscious of Hilde Kornbluth looking at him.

'I am afraid that someone from London could not possibly match the standards of Vienna,' he said.

'But you could try,' said Hilde, taking him firmly by the hand.

Seymour was not a good dancer but Hilde and the music swept him round in a manner which he thought reasonably satisfactory.

'You like it, yes?' said Hilde.

'Carried away,' said Seymour.

And, indeed, it would be very easy to be carried away. For Seymour, new to the dance and unused to the style of dancing, there was something infectious and heady about it. The closeness of Hilde's body, the abandon and gaiety of the rhythm, the heavy scent of the flowers and what seemed to Seymour the general surrender, made it all more than mildly intoxicating.

For Hilde, however, the experience was perhaps less satisfactory and after a few turns on the floor she led him back to the table, where Kornbluth was now surrounded by a group of acquaintances.

Seymour was chatting on the edge of the circle when he felt himself tapped on the back. He turned round and saw Maddalena.

'So,' she said, 'you have abandoned us for Vienna.'

Chapter Seven

'Not so,' said Seymour. 'I am merely dallying with Vienna. My heart remains elsewhere.'

'Ah, yes,' said Maddalena, 'Vienna invites dalliance. That is what the music says, Lehar's music, anyway. But do not be deceived. The light foot can wear a heavy boot.'

She linked her arm through his.

'I have come to take you away,' she said. 'I think you are in danger.'

He had expected her to lead him to the artists' table but she did not. Instead, she took him to the top of the piazza and then out into the streets beyond it.

'Where are you going?' he said.

'Home.'

'Your home?'

'Yes. I have one.'

Their way took him through the Piazza Giovanni, where Maddalena stopped in front of the marble figure of the composer, Verdi.

'Shall I tell you something?' she said. 'This is where the Austrians wished to erect a statue of the Emperor. But the Italians here would not have it. They put this statue here instead. Not just because Verdi is Trieste's greatest composer but because of what his music says. It speaks of protest and revolt. *Nabucco* is the opera of what we call the Risorgimento, the uprising, the revolt. Rebellion against Austrian rule. It puts into music everything we Italians feel. For Italians, opera is their voice, the only voice of theirs that until recently has been able to be heard. On the Emperor's birthday we show our protest by singing *Nabucco*. Oh, the Austrians play other music. They have their bands, their military bands. But the sound of their military music cannot drown Verdi, because Verdi's music is the music of our hearts.'

She gestured towards the statue.

'I tell you this so that you will not waste your time dallying with the music of Lehar. Lehar is frivolity, escape, deception. It says that life is gaiety, all dancing beneath the trees. Forget, it says, forget the rest. There is just the moment floating like a bubble. But Verdi says: Remember. Remember, do not ever forget. Do not be tricked, do not be lured away. Remember, always. Remember.'

She laughed.

'Do you know what the Italians say about Verdi? That even his name is patriotic. What do the letters spell? V for Vittorio, E for Emanuel, Re d'Italia. Victor Emanuel, King of Italy. Italy. He is our true king, not the Emperor of the Austrians. It is on his birthday that we all wear flowers in our buttonholes. But on the birthday of the Emperor there is nothing, no flowers in buttonholes, no flags on the houses. The only flags are on public buildings. By order.'

She laughed again.

'And do you know where in the end they had to put the Emperor's statue? In the Post Office!'

In the morning Maddalena looked out of the window and then beckoned to Seymour.

'Look!' she said.

Seymour looked out of the window and saw the man in the trilby hat.

'He has been there all night. I hope,' said Maddalena, with satisfaction.

Seymour felt uneasy. It was uncomfortable having his behaviour observed so precisely. There was something distasteful in the thought that someone, Schneider, perhaps, knew so much about him.

Another thought struck him. How would it look if this were reported back to London? He could just hear that older man saying 'A woman!' in the disdainful way in which he had said 'Drink' of Lomax. He told himself robustly that, actually, they probably wouldn't care a toss. All the same, he didn't like feeling that he had given away a certain purchase over himself.

'Go on standing there!' instructed Maddalena.

She had taken up a sketch-pad and was sitting on the bed sketching him.

He felt embarrassed and shifted uneasily.

'Don't move!' said Maddalena. 'It won't take a minute.'

Down below in the street Trilby, too, stirred uncomfortably under Seymour's apparent gaze. After a moment he moved away.

'Stay still!' order Maddalena.

'I feel captive,' complained Seymour.

'That's right.'

'What do you mean: "right"?'

'That's how I feel all the time in Trieste,' said Maddalena.

Despite himself, Seymour, as he walked back to the Consulate, found himself thinking about Maddalena. Despite himself because it was out of character. Perhaps because of his immigrant background – no time off if you're an immigrant! – Seymour was regrettably single-minded about his work, to an extent that his colleagues found off-putting. He focused on it to the extinction of all else, which was splendid, as his mother frequently pointed out, for his employers but less splendid when it came to other things.

Chief of these in her mind was the all-important issue of grandchildren. As the years went by she became increasingly concerned that she might have another one like her daughter on her hands. It wasn't that Seymour didn't like women; it was just that when he was busy they somehow slipped to the periphery of his attention.

Maddalena, however, stubbornly refused to slip. Now, as he walked back through the sun-soaked streets, he was conscious of her physically to an extent that surprised him. He was aware of how she had felt in his arms, the pressure of her body, the smell of her hair. And then there was the impact of her personality, which stayed with him, almost bruisingly, long after he had left her apartment.

Partly it was that she was so different from anyone he had previously met. She was somehow freer. In the East End, or at any rate in the immigrant part of it, girls were surprisingly strait-laced. You were always conscious of the pressure of the community. If you just stopped to talk to a girl in the street, Jesus, the next moment it was all round the neighbourhood and by the time you got home your mother had about ordered the wedding cake!

He had expected it to be much the same in Trieste. Before he had left, old Angelinetti had called him aside. 'Now, son . . .' and warned him about meddling with wives, daughters, etc. 'It's different there, son, it's the family honour, you see . . .' Nevertheless, he had admitted there were exceptions.

Maddalena, Seymour supposed, was one of the exceptions. That was probably because she was an artist, or moved in those circles. Seymour didn't know much about artists, had never really met any before he came to Trieste. From what he had seen, they were all right, if slightly crazed, but, on the whole, people it was best to steer a little clear of.

And that probably went for Maddalena, too. He could see that she wasn't exactly the sort of woman a British Consul should be pally with. Nor a Special Branch officer seconded on special duty, either.

Yet he couldn't get her out of his mind. She challenged him. She wasn't at all what he expected a woman to be. He could see, in his more detached moments, that this was as much to do with what he was as with what she was, and with his own background in a strongly traditional, rather rigid immigrant community in which the role of a woman was heavily circumscribed. But, hell, he was moving

92

beyond that kind of community, that was the past, he wasn't like his Mum and Dad; it couldn't just be that.

Anyway, he ought not to be giving her too much attention. This was just a fling, something on the side, taking place, fortunately, where no one knew him and couldn't report back. (Except that goddamned 'shadow' that was perpetually behind him, but, luckily, this was not the sort of thing he and his superiors would be interested in, and if report got back, it certainly wouldn't be to his mother.)

No, the important thing, he told himself sternly, was that he should be concentrating on his work. This was a career opportunity for him, the first real one that he had had; and he must not let it slip. This, of all times, was not the one to allow himself to be distracted.

There was, besides, a strong particular reason for not allowing himself to get too close to Maddalena. It was abundantly clear that she identified herself strongly with the Italian cause in the maelstrom of national politics that was Trieste. And if Lomax, as was beginning to seem not at all unlikely, had come to grief because he had allowed his sympathies to carry him too far, then the most likely object of them that Seymour had seen up till now had been the Italians.

On his way back, he went past the Edison and that brought into his mind his visit there the other evening. The pickets were no longer in evidence. Of course they would only be there in the evening, when there was a showing. The thought came to him that because of that Kornbluth might have missed them. Anyway, it was worth a try.

The newspaper seller was there at his post.

'Still here, then?'

'I am always here.'

'Always? Even when the cinema comes out?'

'That's bloody midnight! I've got a wife, you know. Or will have, if we get round to the church some time. It's got

93

to be a church, she says. No registry office for her! And she's a good Socialist too! I tell you, it shocks me.'

'So you're not here, then, when the cinema comes out?' said Seymour, disappointed.

'I go home when the pickets come.'

'You don't picket, yourself?'

'Well, I do, as a matter of fact. But only when people are going in. After that I go home, because Maria cooks a good meal for me and if I'm not there to enjoy it, she kicks hell out of me.'

'Do you know someone I could speak to who is normally there at the end?'

'You could try Pietro, I suppose,' said the newspaper seller.

Pietro was in the local office of the Socialist Party; and the office was in a shabby street where women sat in the doorways and waif-like children stared at him with bucket eyes. It consisted of a single room. Newspapers such as the newspaper seller sold, that is, radical ones, and leaflets such as Seymour had seen being distributed at the Canal Grande, were piled everywhere. The Trieste Socialists were strong on paper if not on much else.

Pietro sat behind a small table, smoking.

'You could try Paulo,' he said.

Paulo was to be found down at the docks. Several other men, equally shabby, were to be found with him, sitting in the shade with their backs against a wall. Evidently the port's prosperity had not extended universally.

'Yes, I'm Paulo,' he said defiantly. 'And yes, I was on picket at the Edison.'

'And so was I,' said someone else. 'And what has that got to do with you?'

'It means you may be able to help me,' said Seymour.

'Why should we help you?'

'What does it cost to help?' asked Seymour.

94

It was a saying from the Triestino. They registered it but, coming from someone like him, it made them uneasy.

'Who are you?' one of them said.

Seymour thought for a second, then said:

'I am English.'

There could be advantages, given the usual Trieste tensions, in not falling into the usual Triestian categories.

They drew away from him however.

'We cannot help you,' one of them said.

They looked away with studied indifference.

Seymour, though, had grown up among docks people. He squatted down beside them with his back against the wall.

After a while, someone said:

'Are you going to go away?'

'No.'

The man shrugged.

'Stay, then.'

It made them uncomfortable, however. He knew they wouldn't be able to stay silent for long.

'Aren't you afraid you will dirty that posh suit?' someone taunted him.

'No.'

'Look, why don't you just push off?'

'I need your help.'

'Well, we're not going to give it you.'

Seymour continued to sit there.

One of them got up and came and stood in front of him.

'Bugger off!' he said threateningly.

Seymour looked up at him.

'When you have told me what I want,' he said; watching the man's boots, however.

'Shall I kick his head in?' the man asked the others.

'What does it cost to help?' Seymour said again.

'This man's getting on my nerves.'

'He's getting on all our nerves.'

'Just who the hell are you?'

'I've told you. I'm English. And I want some information about an Englishman who died.'

'You'd better go to the police, then.'

'Would *you* go to the police?'

There was a short silence and then, as Seymour had counted on, a general laugh.

'Yes, but why come to us?'

'I think you might be able to help me. You see, the Englishman went to the Edison the night he was killed. It was one of the nights you were picketing on.'

'We don't know anything about it.'

'Well, I think you might. He went in with a friend. A tall Irishman. Now, what I want to know is what happened when they came out. I think you could have seen them.'

'A lot of people came out.'

'Two foreigners.' He had a moment of inspiration. 'Talking.'

There was a slight flicker of amusement.

'Everyone talks,' said Paulo, though.

'Not like this. They were talking like *professori*. And they would have been talking in English.'

'They shouldn't have been there. What the hell do you think we go picketing for?'

'They were foreigners. It wasn't their business.'

'Well, they're not our business.'

'A dead man is everyone's business.'

It was another Triestino saying; and here, again, was the one he had used before.

'What, after all, does it cost to help?'

'What do you want to know?' someone said.

'What happened when they came out.'

'Nothing happened. They talked, like you said.'

'And then?'

'The Irishman went away.'

'We know the Irishman,' someone said.

'He teaches at the People's University in the evenings.'

'It's the other one I want to know about. What did he do? Did he go off by himself? Did he meet someone? Was he going to meet someone?'

'He didn't need to.'

'I'm sorry?'

'He didn't need to go anywhere. The person he was meeting was inside.'

'Inside the cinema?'

'That's right.'

'Just a minute,' said Seymour. 'Let's get this clear. He came *out* of the cinema. With the Irishman. Are you saying he then went back inside?'

'That's right.'

'After the Irishman had gone?'

'After everyone had gone.'

'Everyone?'

'Everyone. Including the staff. We hang on for them especially. The bastards! They ought to be out with us.'

'So who was he seeing, then?'

'Oh, well. Who's left when everyone else has gone home?'

It was, although he did not know it at the time, yet another Trieste saying. It had been offered offhandedly, as something that hardly needed saying, obvious to anybody. It wasn't obvious to Seymour, however. Spotting that, they seized on it, glad of the opportunity to put the superior outsider at a disadvantage. They had been uneasy about him, unsure whether he was on the side of authority or not. Perhaps they had told him too much. Here, now, was a chance to put that right. They refused to say any more. He had asked for help and they had given it him. Now he had to make of it what he could That was fair, wasn't it?

He walked up from the docks thinking about it. On his way he passed through the Piazza Grande. The man who had joined them the other day, the friendly one, Ettore, was sitting alone in the Café of Mirrors. He looked up at Seymour and smiled.

'I know!' he said. 'I'm early. I ought not to be here till later. In fact, I am not here. It is an illusion created by the

97

café's mirrors. Really I am at work. However, the meeting finished early and on my way back to the office, smelling the coffee . . .'

He was smoking, as, going by the other day, he seemed to do all the time. Seymour sat down to windward of him. Ettore noticed and waved a hand apologetically.

'It is bad,' he said, 'I know. I am trying to stop. I have spoken to my analyst about it – did you know, I go to a psychoanalyst regularly? I said: "How can you claim to put the big things right when you cannot put the small things right?" "Who says they are the small things?" he replied.'

Seymour laughed.

'For me, it is coffee,' he said. 'We all have our vices.'

'For everyone it is coffee,' said Ettore. 'But in my case that is, too.'

Seymour asked him how he had come to know Lomax. Through James, Ettore said. One day after their English lesson he had brought Ettore to the table in the Café of Mirrors and Lomax had been there. They had not met through business. His father-in-law normally handled the foreign side. Seymour rather gathered the impression that in anything to do with work Ettore was dominated by his father-in-law. He suspected that part of the attraction for Ettore of opening a branch in England was the prospect of getting away from him.

They talked a little about life in England. It was the first time Seymour had had much of a talk with Ettore and he found him not just sympathetic but also vaguely comforting. It was a relief to find someone fairly normal at the artists' table. Then he remembered that Ettore was himself an artist; at any rate, he wrote novels. He asked Ettore about that. Ettore said that his early novels had had such a hammering from critics, mostly on the grounds that, coming from Trieste, he couldn't write proper Italian, that he had virtually given up.

Seymour had an idea.

'Ettore, as a Triestian, could you give me some advice? It is about the meaning of what I gather is an old Trieste

98

saying. Who is left behind when everyone else has gone home?'

'Are you getting at me?'

'No,' said Seymour, surprised.

'It is what my father-in-law is always saying to me. Pointedly. When I leave work at what I think is a reasonable time.'

'Why? Who *is* left?'

'The boss. It is a Trieste saying, I think a foolish one. However, it is very popular with small businessmen.'

If he remembered rightly, the boss at the Edison, from what James had said, was a man named Machnich. Who also happened to be the person James had had dealings with over the venture of starting up cinemas in Ireland, if that had actually happened. And also the person, if James's rambling account could be trusted, to whom Lomax had given business advice. Seymour thought it was time he looked at those dealings a little more closely.

When Seymour got back to the Consulate, he asked Koskash if there was any record of the occasions on which Lomax had offered help to James Juice and also, possibly, to some Trieste businessmen, over setting up a cinema in Ireland.

'Oh, yes,' said Koskash, 'there's a big file.'

He brought it in and gave it to Seymour.

Seymour began to work through it. Lomax's contributions appeared to be almost entirely technical and legal. He advised on Irish Customs regulations and on necessary licences and permits. On how to secure local banking facilities, on things to be borne in mind when renting premises, on employment law in Ireland. He seemed to know a lot about it; not just the theoretical requirements but how they were translated into practice on the ground. Reading it, Seymour was impressed. So far he had been inclined to dismiss Lomax as just an advanced nut. Going through what Lomax had written, however, he found a sharp, practical mind at work. It was a new side of Lomax that he was seeing. What was it that Koskash had said? That they had all said. That he was actually very good at his job.

And his role appeared to have been confined to giving advice. There was no hint that he had been involved in any other way, no hint of any personal financial involvement, for example, as Seymour had half suspected there might be. The actual financial side of it wasn't, in fact, at all clear. But so far as James personally was concerned the financial arrangements *were* clear. They were contained in some separate pencilled notes. It looked as if as well as providing general advice to the group of Trieste businessmen behind the enterprise, Lomax had been giving James some private advice on the side. There was nothing underhand, just a few practical points, offered as a friend, that James should bear in mind. Advice probably much needed, thought Seymour.

It was beginning to fall into place now; a man with actually a good business idea – surprisingly – approaching a group of businessmen for backing. And then, gradually, the more astute backers taking over and the original visionary somehow getting lost to view. James, as he had said, had had the imagination; but not, Seymour suspected, any practical business or political sense at all.

Lomax had eventually had both of these and, reading between the lines, Seymour thought he could see him offering advice fairly to the Trieste businessmen but at the same time trying gently to see that James didn't get taken for too much of a ride.

The principal backer appeared to be, as James had said, Machnich.

'The owner of the Edison?'

'That is right, yes,' said Koskash. 'And much else in Trieste besides. His principal business is a large carpet shop.'

'What sort of man is he?'

'What sort of man?' Koskash grimaced. 'A businessman of the Trieste variety. That is to say, at heart, small. His business is big now but he likes to run everything as if he was still running a small shop. He has to know everything, almost do everything, for himself. As soon as he can't, he begins to get nervous. That, I think, may be why the Dublin venture never came to anything. He has a big idea and then the bigness of the idea frightens him.'

Even so, thought Seymour, the sort of man who would eat James alive. And Lomax too? Not if Schneider were to be believed and not on the evidence of the notes in this file. On this evidence, Lomax was a sharp customer.

When he had finished going through the file Seymour closed it and put it away in the out-tray and sat thinking. He thought for quite a while and then made up his mind. There was something he had to do and he might as well do it now.

He went into the front office where Koskash was at his desk working and then pulled up a chair and sat down exactly in front of him.

'Koskash,' he said, 'it is time we had a talk.'

'Certainly,' said Koskash, putting down his pen.

'Koskash,' said Seymour, 'you have not been entirely honest with me.'

'Haven't I?' said Koskash, surprised. 'I am sorry you should think that.'

'That man the other night, the one I gave the papers to: he wasn't a seaman, was he?'

'Wasn't he?'

'He wasn't British, was he? This is the British Consulate and you would only have power to issue papers to British nationals.'

'Not necessarily. If they are crewing on British ships –'

'I looked at your copy, Koskash. It was made out as for a British national. Why was that, Koskash?'

'I – I do not know.'

'You lied to me, Koskash. You knew he wasn't a seaman.'

Koskash looked uncomfortable.

'I am sorry,' he said.

'Who was he, Koskash?'

Koskash shook his head.

'I am afraid I cannot say,' he said.

'This won't do, Koskash. I'm afraid you have to say. This is the British Consulate and the man wasn't British. You were issuing British papers to a man who wasn't British. And not even a seaman. Why was that, Koskash? Why did you do it? Was it for money?'

Koskash jumped as if he had been stung.

'No!' he said. 'No. Not that, never! I would never do a thing like that for money!'

'Then why, Koskash?'

Koskash just shook his head.

'I am sorry,' he said. 'I am very sorry.'

'I am afraid, Koskash, that I need to know.'

He waited.

'Shall I help you? What I think you were doing was helping someone to leave the country, someone who couldn't leave the country in the ordinary way. I wonder why that was? I can only think, Koskash, that it was because the authorities were looking for him. Was that what it was, Koskash?'

He waited, but Koskash did not reply. He just shook his head faintly from side to side.

'They could leave the country only under a false identity, and that you were willing to provide for them. You could give them false papers, papers which would enable them to get on a ship. Why, Koskash, why were you doing that?'

Koskash found his tongue.

'I am sorry,' he said. 'I am truly very sorry. But I cannot tell you that.'

'But you must, Koskash. Otherwise I may have to go to the authorities. Mr Kornbluth, say, or, more probably, to Mr Schneider.'

Koskash closed his eyes as if in pain but shook his head again dumbly.

'I do not want to do that, Koskash, but I am afraid I may

102

have to. If you won't tell me anything. You have been abusing the trust Mr Lomax placed in you.'

'No!' said Koskash.

'But yes! This is the British Consulate. The *British*. And you have been issuing false papers under its name. You have been taking advantage of your position here for purposes of your own.'

'No,' said Koskash. 'I would not do that. I would never do that. It would not be honourable,' he said earnestly.

'But, Koskash, that is exactly what you *have* been doing. You have been making out papers secretly –'

'No!' said Koskash hoarsely.

Seymour stopped.

'No?'

'No.'

'Are you saying,' said Seymour slowly, 'that you were *not* doing this secretly?'

'That is right, yes. I was not doing it secretly.'

'What are you saying, Koskash? That Mr Lomax *knew* what you were doing?'

'That is so, yes.'

For a moment Seymour couldn't think what to say.

'You surprise me, Koskash.'

'I know. It *is* surprising,' said Koskash simply. 'But it is true.'

'He knew what you were doing? And didn't stop it?'

Koskash nodded.

'How far was Mr Lomax involved in this? In what you were doing? This . . . arrangement? He knew what you were doing. Was there more to it than that?

Koskash shook his head.

'He knew what I was doing,' he said hoarsely. 'That is all.'

'He knew, but condoned it. Is that what you are saying?'

'That is what I am saying,' said Koskash quietly.

Chapter Eight

'Sand.'

'– or,' said Seymour.

The man at the Club's reception desk raised his head.

'Or what, sir?'

'Sandor. That's the name. S-a-n-d-o-r. Sandor. It's a Hungarian name. Comes from my mother.'

'Right, sir. Thank you, sir. Well, Mr Sandor, if you'll just –'

'That's just my first name. You said you wanted my full name.'

'Well, yes, sir. If you wouldn't mind.'

'Pelczynski.'

'Pel . . .?'

Resignedly Seymour spelt it out.

'It's a Polish name. Comes from my grandfather.'

Why did he have to go on like that? He knew why. Ever since he had started going to school he had been self-conscious about his name. Most of the teachers in the East End were used to the assortment of immigrant names but it so happened that his first teacher had not been; and floundered.

'Pel . . .' Mumble, mumble. 'Well, thank you, sir, I'll –'

'Seymour.'

And even that had problems. 'Listen,' his grandfather had said when he got to England. 'No Englishman is ever going to get his jaw round a name like Pelczynski!' And he had changed it to Seymour, retaining, however, Pelczynski as a second Christian name in the family to the chagrin of his descendants ever since.

'Sandor Pelczynski Seymour,' said Seymour firmly.

'Right, sir. Thank you, sir. If you'll just take a seat, I'll tell Mr Barton that you're here.'

So Seymour sat down on the horsehair-stuffed, leather-upholstered sofa in the foyer of the English Club and waited. Seymour wasn't used to clubs. Ordinary police-men from the East End weren't. But he had been in one once, taken in by a superior when he was one of the team working on the Ripper case in Whitechapel not long before. Seymour's job had been to check out some of the royal suspects. Well, that had been a waste of time. He had run straightaway into the same wall of superiority and superciliousness, call it class distinction if you liked, that he had encountered when he had gone to the Foreign Office. The English Club in Trieste wasn't quite like that but it had something of the same air as the club he had been taken to in the West End. 'Neutral ground,' his superior had said. Well, it wasn't neutral ground as far as Seymour was concerned.

There were the same comfortable chairs, the same dis-creet, deferential servants. From a room in the back he could hear the click of billiard balls. English newspapers were strewn on the tables and there was a rack of illus-trated periodicals hanging from the wall. While he was watching, a man came in and took one. He went into an inner room, where Seymour caught a glimpse of yet more comfortable chairs. 'Surrey, 231 for one,' the man said to someone already sitting there.

On the wall were pictures of hunting scenes, together with a portrait of the monarch: not, actually, the present King but the old Queen, Victoria. The English Club in Trieste, like most clubs, in Seymour's view, was a bit behind the times.

Barton came bustling in.

'Seymour! Good to see you. Good of you to come.'

'It was kind of you to invite me.'

'I thought, just while you're here – I know it probably won't be for long, but even so, I thought you'd be glad of the chance to get back to a piece of England occasionally.'

'I would indeed,' said Seymour untruthfully.

Barton led him into the inner room, the reading room perhaps, and took him over to a corner, away from the only two other inhabitants.

'Tea? Or something stronger?'

'Coffee?'

'Coffee it is.' Barton went off to place the order, then came back and sat down opposite him.

'Well, how are you finding things? And how are you getting on with sorting things out over poor old Lomax?'

'Oh, reasonably well. People are very helpful'

'Well, of course, they are. In Trieste. Usually.'

'As a matter of fact, though, there's one area where I could do with a bit of help. The business side. I thought you might be able to help me.'

'Well, of course. Only too glad to.'

'It's really to do with the cinema.'

'Cinema!'

'Don't you know about it? I thought you might have heard.'

'Did hear something about it. Jog my memory.'

'There's an Irishman who wanted to start up some cinemas in Dublin and persuaded some Trieste businessmen to join him. Lomax gave them some advice. You know, help on Customs, that sort of thing.'

'Irishman? That man, Juice?'

'That's right.'

'I'd steer clear of him if I were you. He's a bit of a nutcase.'

'I know, I know. Perhaps that's the reason why Lomax was helping him. Hold his hand, you know. See he didn't get into too deep water.'

106

'That man would be out of his depth in a bloody puddle.'

'And he was in it, you see, with some quite sharp people. Do you know a fellow named Machnich?'

'The carpet shop?'

'And cinemas, apparently.'

'Has trouble with his people. Hasn't he got a strike on?'

'Yes. What is it about?'

'The usual. Wages. Hours. Bringing in people who work for less.'

'Bringing in? Immigrants?'

'We don't call them that. There's so much coming and going of people in the Empire, and certainly in Trieste. But yes. People he brought in from outside. His own kind usually.'

'A tough customer, is he?'

'Too tough for Juice, definitely. But I don't know how tough he'd be if it really came to it. They say he's going to settle.'

'And what about Lomax? Is he up to mixing it with someone like Machnich?'

'I don't know that a consul usually needs to mix it,' said Barton doubtfully. 'It's usually just a case of giving advice. Actually, from what I heard, they got on surprisingly well.'

'Surprisingly?'

'Well, you know, they used to go off for a drink together. But he never came here for a drink. He'd drink with a foreigner but not with us. I call that surprising.'

It was true about the strike. In the piazza outside the Edison there was surprising activity this morning. Men were spilling out of the taverna and then standing talking. One of them looked up as Seymour went by.

'Christ, here he is again!'

107

Seymour glanced at him and thought he recognized him.

'What is it this time?' said another voice resignedly.

This time he did recognize the man. He was one of the men he had talked to down in the docks.

'Hello!' he said. 'What are you doing up here?'

'What do you think we're doing?' said the first man bitterly. Seymour had placed him now. It was the most aggressive of the dockers, the one who had threatened to kick him. 'Giving in, of course.'

'Giving in?'

'It's all over. She's bloody fixed it. Fixed it with that bastard, Machnich.'

'The strike? You're going back to work?'

'*They're* going back to work. We're bloody not.'

'I suppose it's good from their point of view,' said another man.

'Well, yes, they'll be able to start collecting their pay packet again, won't they? But it won't be any bigger. Or not much. They ought to have held out. As it is, all they've done is lose money.'

'They say it wasn't about money. It was about conditions.'

'It's always about money!' said the first man derisively.

'It seems a pity,' said another man, 'after we'd shown solidarity.'

'That's it! And that's the trouble with getting a woman involved. They're too ready to do a deal. What the hell are we doing, letting a woman represent us?'

'She's got the gift of the gab,' said someone doubtfully.

'Well, yes, and that worries me sometimes. You never know where these people are leading us.'

'You ought to be doing that, Benito.'

'Leading? Me? Christ, no! Stick your head out and yours is the first head that gets chopped.'

'It doesn't seem to worry her.'

'Well, it ought to. And she oughtn't to be so ready to do deals.'

'I wouldn't call her soft,' said another of the men, who hadn't so far spoken.

'Well, I wouldn't call her soft. But she gets on a bit too well with that bastard, Machnich.'

'Fowl of a kind, I suppose.'

'That's it! That's just it! The whole point of the Party is to get past divisions of that kind, Italian against Serb, Slovenian against Austrian. But she's going back to it.'

'So it's all over?' said Seymour.

'All over. The men at the carpet shop have gone back. They've got no need for us now. "Thanks very much, mate." "Thank *you*. But what about a bit of solidarity? We showed solidarity with you and it put a bit more in your pay packet. But we haven't *got* any pay packets. How about showing a bit of solidarity with us?" "Ah, well, that's different . . ." Too bloody true it's different. And that's why they shouldn't have accepted. And why she shouldn't have done a deal.'

'I don't know what I shall do tonight.' said another man. 'Not with no picket line to be on. It gave a bit of point to things.'

The groups outside the taverna were breaking up and dispersing.

'What shall we do now?'

'Back to the docks, I suppose.'

'How about a drink?' suggested Seymour. 'I'll stand you one. I owe you something for your help.'

'Well . . .'

They looked at each other.

'We sort of know him now,' said one of the men hesitantly.

'A drink is real, even if friendship is not,' said Seymour, finding from somewhere at the back of his mind one of old Angelinetti's sayings.

'Well, that is true.'

They didn't go back into the taverna because it was still full, but chose another up one of the side streets, where they stood at the counter and the bar tender drew the wine from barrels.

'So it helped you a bit?' one of them said, looking at Seymour curiously.

'A bit. Not as much as I'd have liked, but that's not your fault.'

'You worked it out, did you?'

'Slowly. Machnich.'

'Yes, Machnich. What they were up to in there together, God alone knows.'

'Another of Machnich's pies. They say he's got a finger in every pie in Trieste.'

'Two big for his boots, that bastard.'

'They do say, though, that he looks after his own.'

'Yes, but that's what I'm complaining of. He looks after his own, but how about everyone else?'

'Those bastards in the Edison never came out.'

'I wish Machnich had come out. Come out of the cinema, that is, and tried to cross our line. I'd have given him a mouthful. But he never showed himself. Not once!'

'He didn't need to. He's got another door. A private one. It lets you on to the Piazza delli Cappucine out the back. Not this piazza. He had it put in in case of emergencies.'

'Just the sort of sneaky thing he would do. Why didn't he come out and face us man to man?'

'Well, that's just the sort of thing these big blokes never do. They always leave that bit to someone else.'

They finished their drink and thanked him politely. However, they refused another one. Seymour, used to the ways of dock people, could understand that.

Going back through the Piazza Grande, he found the artists, as ever, at their table. Did they do nothing but drink? Evidently they did, because Alfredo called up at him:

'Are you coming this evening?'

'Coming? What to?'

'James is giving a lecture.'

'Oh, really? What on?'

'Ireland,' said James. 'Ireland and Trieste.'

'Sort of . . .' Seymour hesitated. '. . . geographical?'

'Cultural,' said James. 'And political.'

'Oh, yes?'

'What I shall bring out,' said James, 'are the similarities between Ireland and Trieste.'

'Really?'

'Yes. Both are oppressed nations struggling to be free.'

'Yes, yes. I suppose you could say that.'

'Trieste is certainly struggling to be free,' said Lorenzo. 'But is it a nation?'

'Part of a nation,' said James.

'But which nation?'

'Italy, of course.'

'And Ireland?'

'Struggling to be free from England,' said James. 'And the Church.'

'Well, that's a problem here, too, of course.'

'Exactly! What I shall say is –'

Seymour began to move away.

'You will come, won't you?' said Alfredo coaxingly.

'I'll certainly try to.'

'The People's University. At eight.'

When Seymour got to the Consulate, he found Mrs Koskash there as well as Koskash. They seemed to have been having an argument. Mrs Koskash was flushed and tight-lipped, Koskash grim. They both greeted him, however, politely.

'I mustn't stay, though,' said Mrs Koskash. 'There are dozens of things I have to do.'

She bustled out.

Koskash stood for a moment looking at her retreating back, then turned away.

'She is always busy,' he said quickly to Seymour. 'She

111

does so many things in the community. For so many causes.'

'Bazaars,' said Seymour, remembering his sister. 'Cake sales. Street collections.'

'Why, yes,' said Koskash, surprised. 'That's right.'

The thought of his sister brought to Seymour's mind the occasions on which he had last seen Mrs Koskash.

'Your wife's a Socialist, isn't she?'

'Yes,' said Koskash. 'Does that matter?'

'Not at all,' said Seymour. 'My own sister is one.'

'She is? I am one myself, of course, although not as committed as she is. She is the chairman of our branch.'

'Ah! Then she, perhaps, is the person who has been negotiating on behalf of the strikers at Machnich's carpet shop?'

'Yes, that's right. They had a long session last night. It is being put to the vote this morning.'

'It's been put to the vote. They've accepted.'

'Well, that is probably good,' said Koskash. 'They've been out for a long time.'

'Your wife is evidently a formidable lady.'

'Yes, indeed. Yes, indeed.'

He settled himself at his desk.

'I have quite a bit of work to do,' he said. 'I shall probably stay on late this evening, if that is all right.'

Seymour was surprised the work was there. But then, with Lomax missing, Koskash was probably doing his work as well. He wondered uneasily if he ought to be doing something about the general work of the Consulate: but that, he decided, was something for Lomax's superiors in London to see to. They would have heard of his death by now.

Koskash was hesitating.

'Will you, yourself, be here this evening?'

'No, probably not. I may go to a lecture at the People's University.'

'Ah, really?'

'Given by Mr Juice.'

'I have been to some of his lectures before. He is usually very good. Odd, but good. Different from the other lecturers, anyway. Yes, you should go. You will find it entertaining.'

Seymour was less sure about that but felt a certain degree of curiosity. He might well go.

He went back into the inner room. The heavy and mostly empty appointments book was on top of the desk. He began to go systematically through the pages. What he was looking for was any reference to the Casa Revoltella. There was one, for the day of the reception, and it was underlined. It was one of the few entries that Lomax had made for himself. The entries at the beginning of the book had been made, dutifully, by Koskash, but after a while he had given up, switching instead to the bits-of-paper prompting that Koskash had told Seymour about. The reception had evidently become important to Lomax for some reason: perhaps the reason that Maddalena had suggested, that something in connection with it had disrupted what appeared to be the even flow of his existence.

Some person. In his investigation so far Seymour was very short of individual names. He had been looking for them all the time. This seemed to be a chance of getting one. At least there *was* an individual here, if Maddalena was to be believed, and he saw no reason why she shouldn't be.

But the name. That was what Maddalena had come looking for and what he, Seymour, was looking for now. He went through the pages without success and then asked Koskash, who couldn't help him. If Lomax had made any appointment with whoever it was, that hadn't been registered in Koskash's system.

Had Lomax *mentioned* a name? Koskash couldn't recall any of particular significance at that time. He showed Seymour his notes, which were, as Seymour had come to expect, detailed and meticulous. The only names were those of officials. Seymour asked about them. It was possible, wasn't it, that an official might wish to go to the reception, either through vanity or in the hope of an informal way of doing business? But no, the officials Koskash mentioned would all have had more promising means of getting invited to the reception than going through Lomax.

Seymour realized he would have to go back to his starting point: Maddalena.

It suddenly struck him that he didn't know where to look for her. He could go to the artists' table, of course, but he wanted to talk to her away from all the others. He was still leaving open the possibility of an Italian dimension to Lomax's sympathies. Where else could she be? How did she spend her days? She modelled, of course, and might be with some artist or other, but if she was, he wouldn't have a hope of finding her. Almost on the off-chance, he went back to her apartment, where, slightly to his surprise, he found her.

She seemed pleased to see him; more than pleased, delighted. He felt a twinge of contrition. He really ought to have gone back to her before this, carried things on somehow from where they had been left off. But then, he reminded himself, he had resolved to keep his distance from her. What was all that, he said to himself sternly, about focusing on his work? Why was he here? But this *was* work, a voice within him said. 'Oh, yes?' said another voice, which Seymour firmly suppressed.

He said that he had wondered if she would be out modelling.

'If only,' said Maddalena, with a sigh.

'Not much demand?'

'Not much money.'

He asked her how she spent her days and had a sudden pang at the thought that she might spend them like this. Here. Perhaps that was why she went down to the artists' table. What was it that she had said when she was talking

114

about Lomax? That a woman on her own could feel very alone in Trieste.

'In the library,' said Maddalena.

'In the –?'

Maddalena looked embarrassed.

'Well, I do,' she said defensively. 'I go there most days. It's a very good library.'

'What do you read?'

She looked self-conscious again.

'Everything,' she said. 'I'm trying to catch up.'

'Catch up?'

'I come from Puglia,' she said. 'If you knew Puglia, you'd know what I'm talking about. It's one of the poorest parts of Italy. With everything that goes with that. There's nothing there for anyone and least of all for a woman who – who doesn't want to get caught in the trap. You know, five children before you're twenty, old before your time, your husband loses interest in you. I had to get away. I wanted to get away. I wanted all the things I had missed, education, ideas, art, all the things that I thought other people had. Well, of course, they don't, but I thought they had. So I came up north. But you can't go to a college or a university if you've had an education like I had. As I found out. I bummed around for a while and drifted into modelling.

'What I do mostly is read. And listen. Not just to the artists, although they have helped a lot. They are always talking, about ideas and art, things that matter. I talk to students, too. There are a lot of them in Trieste. Usually they go out of town, to places like Bologna, but the cafés are always full of them. And sometimes in the evening I go to lectures myself, at the People's University. It's not really a university, not like theirs, it's for people who can't go to university, workers, women. People like me. But mostly I read.

'Sometimes there are things I don't understand and then I go to the students and they explain them to me. They are very good and usually know more than they pretend.

115

Sometimes they're silly, of course. And sometimes they draw me in. That business with the statue, for instance. It wasn't really an attempt at art. I just said that because I was annoyed with Marinetti. It was just a student prank. I dared them and they dared me.

'A lot of their jokes are like that. Anti-authority, or against the Hapsburg Government. Especially in Trieste, where there's a lot of feeling about Trieste becoming part of Italy. Well, I don't mind that. It seems so obviously right to me. Of course, there are other students too, who don't feel like that. There are all sorts of students here, from all over the Empire. But that makes it more interesting.

'Lomax found them interesting, too. He liked to talk to them. He was like me. He had never been to university himself and envied them. "If I had my time again . . ." he would say, "I think I would have gone to university." But he came from a poor family, did you know that? They couldn't afford it. And, anyway, he said, they'd never heard of it. Wasn't that funny? Just like me. And yet a consul! He used to like to ask the students questions, about their courses and what they were reading and so on.'

'About their political beliefs?'

'Well, you can't get away from that in Trieste,' said Maddalena drily. 'That's what they were talking about most of the time.'

'And what position did he take?'

'Oh, like an uncle. He would listen and laugh, but not nastily. Sympathetically, so that they would go on. But sympathetically only up to a point. "Now, now!" he would say sometimes. "You mustn't blow the world up, or there'll be nothing left for me to stand on."'

'Maddalena,' said Seymour. 'I've come for your help. You said you wanted to help me and I think you can. I have been trying to find, as I think you were trying to find the other day, names. The names of individuals. Or at least *an* individual. So far I have found nothing. I have a feel for his general sympathies, yes; but what about people? Who did he know, talk to? And especially I have been thinking about what you told me about that reception at the Casa Revoltella. I think that could be important and I'd like to know who the person was.'

Maddalena nodded.

'I have been thinking about that, too. Over and over. But, I am sorry, I cannot think of any name. I don't think he ever told me.'

'Maddalena, the thought occurs to me – you said he talked to students, did he talk to some more than others? Are there any he might have talked to about this reception?'

'He certainly talked about it at least once. I heard him. They had invited him to come to something or other and he said, no, he couldn't. He had to go to this reception. He would very much have preferred to go with them, he said, but that kind of thing was unfortunately part of his job. "Go and drink?" they said. "Part of the job?" "Someone's got to do it," he said. They all laughed. "Maybe I'll become a consul," one of them said. "You've got to be born beau-tiful," he said. He was like that. He could get on with people very well, fit himself into the way they talked and behaved. So, yes, he did mention it. But –'

'Would you ask around among your student friends? You see, from what you say, I think it just possible that they might know the person who wanted Lomax to take him to the reception. It could even be a student.'

Maddalena looked doubtful.

'Well, I don't really think they're the sort who would want to –'

'That depends on what they wanted to go for. Suppose they wanted to go for the same reason as you went to the Piazza Giuseppina and messed up that statue? To play a prank? And suppose Lomax found out? That might have been the reason why he didn't want to take them. And if he was a student he would have had to be taken. He wouldn't have been able to get there any other way.'

'Well, it is a thought,' said Maddalena.

'Just a thought, perhaps. But worth trying. If you wouldn't mind.'

'I would be glad to,' said Maddalena, pleased.

And then I would have an excuse for seeing you again, thought Seymour. But that thought, too, he suppressed.

He returned to the Consulate. Koskash was working away earnestly. What on earth did he find to work on? Seymour was not aware of much mail coming in. Paperwork to do with the ships, Seymour supposed.

Or the seamen.

He found an excuse, later, to send Koskash out of the office for a moment and, while he was away, glanced at the papers on his desk. They were, as he had suspected, seamen's papers. There were two sets. He didn't really have time to scrutinize them and wouldn't really have known what to look for if he had. They seemed normal enough. Two ordinary British seamen.

But *British* seamen. He made up his mind to watch out for them when they came to collect the papers.

But then the thought struck him that perhaps he wouldn't be here when they came for them. Suppose they came, as the other one had, late in the evening?

And then he realized. Koskash was staying on this evening, working late. He made up his mind not to go to the lecture after all.

At around eight he went out, telling Koskash that he was going for a meal. Instead, he walked round the block. The trilby hat fell in behind him. Seymour wasn't having any of that. He could do without that this evening. It was easy, with his experience, to shake the man off.

He returned to the Consulate and took up a position in a doorway across the street.

It was getting dark but this evening was still heavy with heat. The breeze, which had been such a feature of earlier evenings, bringing to the streets even up here in the city the smell of sea mixed with the smell of flowers, was absent and there was nothing to stir the air. Around the Consulate the streets were deserted.

The moments went by. It was hot in the doorway. He felt himself sweating and put up his hand to wipe his sweat from running into his eyes.

He heard footsteps. Two men were coming up the street. They went to the side door of the Consulate and knocked quietly. The door was opened by Koskash and the two went in.

Seymour stepped out of his doorway and walked across the street towards the Consulate.

And then, suddenly, there was the piercing blast of a police whistle, very close. It was answered by another, and then another, converging on the door.

The door opened and two men rushed out. They didn't try to run away, however, but stood there, smiling.

The street was suddenly full of policemen. Seymour pushed past them. The door of the Consulate was open and through it Seymour could see Koskash, sitting at his desk, his face buried in his hands.

Chapter Nine

Koskash was taken away by the police; and the next morning Seymour went to the police station to find out what had become of him. He went first to Kornbluth. Kornbluth looked uncomfortable and said: 'It is nothing to do with me.' After a moment he added: 'You will have to see Schneider.' And Seymour realized that this was one which involved the other sort of police. 'There are two sorts of police in Trieste,' Alfredo had said: the ordinary ones, the municipal police, and the special sort that you didn't have in England.

'Yes, we are holding him,' said Schneider.

'On what charges?'

'He has not been charged yet,' said Schneider, 'but they will include committing acts which are against the interests of the State. These are serious charges. And there are others.'

'May I see him?'

'Later.'

'I shall, of course, be sending a report to London.'

'And we shall, of course, be lodging a formal protest about the Consulate's behaviour.'

This, thought Seymour, was looking increasingly like something the Foreign Office was going to have to sort out and not him. In fact, he would need to tread very delicately. If he didn't watch out he would be drawn far beyond any of the roles he was supposed to be filling, whether of King's Messenger or of policeman.

'What would be the nature of your protest?' he asked.

'Allowing diplomatic premises to be used for improper purposes.'

'I am not sure it was allowed. Whatever Koskash was doing, he was doing on his own.'

'Of course you would say that.'

Seymour was silent: because, of course, if what Koskash had said was true, it *had* been allowed: by Lomax.

'I am just a Messenger,' he said, 'and it would not be proper for me to anticipate what my government's response will be.'

'Quite so,' said Schneider.

'I am merely making enquiries so that I can report more accurately what has happened.'

'Of course.'

'Actually, I am not quite sure what *did* happen. Perhaps you can inform me.'

'First,' said Schneider, 'there is something that *you* must explain: your own presence there.'

Seymour hesitated, then decided that nothing was to be lost by telling the truth: up to a point.

'I suspected that something might be occurring that was in need of explanation.'

Schneider nodded.

'We, too. We have been watching the Consulate for some time. There was a suspicion that Consulate staff had been assisting people of interest to us to leave the country illegally. Through the provision of false papers. I arranged for two of my men to present themselves to the Consulate –'

'One moment; not to the Consulate but to a person in the Consulate, who was acting without the Consul's authority.'

'So you say. Yes. However –'

'And when they presented themselves . . .?'

'Papers were issued to them. On that basis I ordered Mr Koskash's arrest.'

'What does he say?'

'Nothing yet. We questioned him last night and we shall continue the questioning this morning.'

'Are you in a position to tell me the identity of the people for whom the papers were being made out? In general terms, that is. Their nationality, for instance.'

'They were Serbs. Students.'

Seymour thought quickly. There was not much he could do about this. In fact, he had better stay out of it. It was definitely something for the Foreign Office to sort out. The only thing in this that concerned him was Lomax's role in it; and, perhaps, the less said about that, the better.

'I am sure London will be as distressed by this incident as I am,' he said smoothly, 'and while I cannot anticipate what they will say, I am confident that they will express their regret that one of their employees, a local employee, of course, should have behaved in such a way.'

He felt slightly uncomfortable saying this. He quite liked Koskash and felt he was letting him down. But he could see no alternative. On this, Koskash was on his own. The most Seymour could do for him – and this was probably in the interests of Britain as well – was to play the thing down. 'While, I am sure, they would not wish to condone the incident, I wonder if it should not be kept in proportion? After all, from what you say, these were only students –'

'Mr Seymour,' said Schneider, 'do you have the faintest idea what you are talking about?'

Seymour swallowed. Perhaps he was not doing as well at the diplomatic business as he had thought he was doing.

'I am, of course,' he said hastily, 'only a Messenger.'

'Yes. So you say. Well, Mr Seymour, here in Trieste students are not, perhaps, as they are in England. They are not schoolchildren. We are not talking about making faces at the teacher or throwing chalk. We are talking about throwing bombs. All across the Empire there have been incidents. And that is reality, Mr Seymour, not vague possibility.'

'But why –'

'Serbian, Mr Seymour. *Serbian*. They were Serbian students.'

'Yes, but –'

Schneider sighed.

'You really do not know, do you? Perhaps you really are just a Messenger. Or perhaps it is Trieste is such a small place to people in London, perhaps they think that it is so small that nothing important can happen there. Well, let me tell you, Mr Seymour, that if they think that, then they are mistaken. Because one thing is bound to another thing and great things are bound to small.'

He stopped and looked at Seymour questioningly.

'You know, at least, that two years ago we took Bosnia under our protection?'

'Of course,' said Seymour, in injured tones, grateful to the newspaper seller for what he had learned from him. 'Everyone knows that!'

'They had, of course, been under our protection for the previous thirty years, but that was by international mandate. It was time to tidy things up. So, as I say, we took them –'

'Over,' said Seymour.

'They joined the Empire. Naturally there were people who were opposed. And not just people, countries. If you can call Serbia a country.'

'Serbia was against it?'

'Violently. In all senses. And especially the young. The students in the universities, the young officers in the army. Passionate without quite knowing what they were being passionate about. Now, of course, there are many students throughout the Empire, students of all nationalities: Hungarian, Slovakian, Montenegrin . . . We pride ourselves on that. And among them are Bosnian students, now part of the Empire, unwillingly, and Serbian students, always likely to cause trouble. So, well, they caused trouble. And, naturally, we have had to crack down on them.'

'I can see that,' said Seymour, 'but why crack down so

123

heavily? Does not that, with the young, lead to more trouble? If you do it with too heavy a hand?'

'Too heavy a hand?' said Schneider, astonished. 'But this is serious, Mr Seymour! We are not talking about regulating football on the playing-fields of Eton. Although from what I hear of English playing-fields . . . No, Mr Seymour, we are talking bombs. Bombs!

'And we are not talking about bombs just in Trieste. Or even Vienna. We are talking about bombs right across Europe. Do you understand that, Mr Seymour? We are talking war. Because, you see, one thing is bound to another, and great things are bound to small. Let us say, for instance, that one day, in some small place, call it Trieste, some foolish student throws a bomb and kills someone important, a Governor, say, or a member of the Royal Family. And suppose we learn that a certain country is responsible. Call it Serbia. Then Austria-Hungary will not take that lying down. They will say to that country: you must do something about this. And if you don't . . .

'And now the problems really start. For Russia says: leave Serbia alone, we will not have this. And Germany, perhaps, says: you keep out of it, we stand by our Hapsburg allies. Countries are bound by treaties. They are obliged to act if the treaty is invoked by some country to which they are allied. One thing is bound to another, great things are sometimes bound to small. A bomb thrown in Trieste could set off a chain of events which could lead to war. Yes, war, Mr Seymour. I see you doubt me. But I am telling the truth, believe me. One little thing could pull in another bigger thing and then another thing. You go down to your taverna at night and you sit drinking and you think the world is secure, safe. There is order and you take it for granted. But I think that peace in Europe is like a house of cards. One card falls and then all the others fall with it.

'So you see, Mr Seymour, this is not a matter of students playing games. They may be playing games, but I am not. I do not want that first card to fall here in Trieste. That first bomb to be thrown. And so . . . so I take students seriously. And especially those students of yours, Mr Seymour. Because I know it is not chalk that they have been getting ready to throw, but something else.'

Seymour walked away from the police station smarting, feeling that he had been given a history lesson which he didn't need. Or perhaps he did need it. International politics hadn't figured high on the curriculum of a policeman in the East End. Nor had Bosnia, Serbia and the rest of them – indeed, the whole Austro-Hungarian Empire – loomed large in what he had done at school. When Seymour had left school at fourteen, the teachers had not yet got round to Bosnia. Of course, he knew something about Central Europe from his work with immigrant families in the East End but there were gaps. Bucovina, for example, where was that? Hands up all those who could place Bucovina!

Not Seymour. He was beginning to regret his lack of knowledge of the international scene. Perhaps he had better get along to the library with Maddalena and do some reading.

But what a load of codswallop it was! All that talk about war! Not a chance, thought Seymour. The sort of rubbish that military-minded people, whether in the army or high up in the police, were always talking. And all that stuff about one thing being bound to another, great things to small! Suppose small things *were* small? Suppose the students *were* just making faces, throwing chalk? Overreacting as Schneider was doing would just make things worse, turn all the Maddalenas into real revolutionaries!

No, it was all codswallop. And probably all Koskash had been doing, out of the misguided goodness of his heart, was giving some naive youngsters a helping hand. It had been wrong of him but not very wrong and Lomax had probably been right to go along with it. From what Maddalena had said, it was the kind of thing that he, with

125

all his evident sympathy for people and underdog causes, would do. Not exactly what he should be doing as Consul, of course, but . . .

All the same, Seymour was uneasy. What was it that Schneider had said at the end? That he *knew* that they were not just chalk throwers. Was that just talk? Or did he really know that? Because if that was indeed the case, then Koskash might have been doing rather more than giving some innocents a helping hand. And if Lomax had condoned it, then, perhaps, he, too, was in a lot deeper than he should have been.

The trouble was that if it was just a question of helping relatively innocent students to escape, Seymour could see no reason why that should have led to Lomax being killed; whereas if Lomax had been involved more deeply in the kind of thing that Schneider was hinting at then Seymour could see quite a few reasons why he might have been.

Yes, there they were again sitting at the table. Didn't they ever do any work? Or were artists in Trieste al fresco too and just sat around drinking? A good life for some, thought Seymour.

Marinetti was handing round some sheets of paper. He gave one to Seymour. Seymour read:

Coffee
Sweet memories frappées
Marmalade of the Glorious Dead
Roast Mummies with Professors' Livers
Archaeological Salad
Stew of the Past, with explosive peas in historical sauce
Fish from the Dead Sea
Lumps of blood in broth
Demolition Starters
Vermouth

'What the hell is this?' he said.

126

'It is the menu for the celebratory dinner after my Futurist Evening,' said Marinetti. 'You, too, are of course invited.'

'Well, thank you. But . . .'

He looked at the menu doubtfully.

'It certainly whets the appetite,' said Luigi; uncertainly, however.

'But why does it do so, in a manner of speaking, back to front? asked Lorenzo.

'Because my Evening will set out to reverse normality,' said Marinetti.

'Oh, I see. Silly of me not to spot it.'

There was a little pause. Then Alfredo said:

'Does that mean that the Future is actually the Past?'

'No, it doesn't,' said Marinetti, annoyed. 'It suggests that we enter the Future by embracing disorder.'

'Oh.'

Then Luigi said:

'But why, in that case, are you having the dinner *after* the Evening? Why not have it before?'

'Because,' said Marinetti, glaring, 'there are dozens of things I still have to do before the Evening can get off the ground. Otherwise there will be bloody chaos!'

Seymour stood there, holding a copy of the menu in his hand, nonplussed.

It was no surprise, when he got back to the Consulate, to find Mrs Koskash standing at the door. He let her in. She was dry-eyed and composed and sat down, apparently relaxed, in the chair he offered.

'Tell me what happened,' she said.

When he had finished, she sat thinking.

'Did they go into the Consulate?' she asked. 'Was he actually inside when they arrested him?'

'They went in,' said Seymour. 'But then he came out. I think he was actually outside when he was formally arrested.'

Mrs Koskash sighed.

'The fool!' she said. 'If he had stayed inside they couldn't have arrested him.'

'I think he may have known that. He said, though, that he had done enough harm to the Consulate as it was.'

Mrs Koskash sighed again. She sat for a moment looking down at her feet.

'I should not have persuaded him,' she said.

'No,' said Seymour. 'And you did persuade him, didn't you? He wouldn't have done it if you hadn't talked him into it. He is not a Serb, after all. But you are, aren't you? And I think you were the one who thought it up. You're practical, aren't you, and committed. You organize things, not just for the Serbs but for the local Socialists. And perhaps others as well.'

'I am active, yes,' said Mrs Koskash. 'A lot of people aren't.'

'And caring, I think. So I think you might well have set up an escape route for dissident Serbs.'

She did not deny it.

'I am sorry about using the Consulate,' she said softly.

'And your husband? What about using him?'

She looked at him hard.

'That is something I have to work out for myself. Perhaps I shall go to them and say: "You have arrested the wrong person. Koskash is not to blame. I am the one you want." However, that is no concern of yours.'

She stood up.

'I have come to ask you for something. It is this. Will you please go and see him in prison? They will agree because you come from the Consulate.'

'I will certainly go and see him.'

'Every day,' she insisted. 'While you are doing that they will not beat him up.'

Seymour was left alone in the Consulate. It suddenly came home to him. He was the only member of the staff left.

128

And he wasn't even, strictly speaking, a member of the staff. A moment of panic seized him. Suppose someone came along wanting the Consulate to do something? Seymour wouldn't be able to do it, that was for sure. He'd have to fob them off, say the Consulate was closed or something. In fact, he'd better put up a notice to that effect right away.

But – just a minute – *could* a Consulate be closed, just like that? Didn't diplomatic representation sort of go on independent of hours? And, anyway, who was Seymour to close a Consulate down? Wait a minute, wait a minute, things were getting out of hand. Jesus, he had only just joined the Diplomatic Service and here he was wanting to close half of it down. Well, not quite half of it. Trieste wasn't quite that important, but it was important, Schneider was not the only one who had said so. Suppose something major blew up? An international crisis or something? Look, hold on, he told himself, you're just an ordinary policeman, you're not the bloody Prime Minister, leave it for him to sort out.

And at that moment there was a knock on the door.

A small boy was standing there. Well, not a small boy, a youth, but dressed in uniform. Someone official, anyway.

'Yes?'

'Are you the Consul?'

'Pretty nearly,' said Seymour.

'Message for you, sir,' said the youth, handing him a letter.

Seymour took it. The boy saluted smartly and moved away.

Seymour looked down at the letter stupidly. It was addressed to him.

But how could it be? It wasn't from his mother or his grandfather and no one outside his family knew he was here. He turned it over and looked at the postmark. Manchester? But he didn't know anyone in Manchester and certainly no one in Manchester knew him. He broke the envelope open. Violet Smethwick? He had never heard of

129

anyone named Smethwick, let alone Violet. Why should anyone named Violet be writing to him? He turned over in his mind, a little uneasily, the various women he had met recently but couldn't place this one.

He started to read the letter and for a moment couldn't make any sense of it at all. And then he realized. Violet. Auntie Vi. Lomax's Auntie Vi!

He stuffed the letter away in his pocket. He'd look at that later. Meanwhile there were more important things to do. He went back to being Foreign Secretary.

No, the first thing to do was notify the Foreign Office in London and suggest *they* did something about it. The second was to modify the notice he had been planning to put up. *Closed* – He crossed that out and altered it. *Temporarily Closed for all but Essential Business.*

And if any of that came along he would refer it to London. That was it! This was beginning to sound like Senior Management. Much more of this and he would declare himself Ambassador.

He put the notice up on the door. If by any chance some business turned up he would make a careful note of it and leave it for someone else to sort out. And meanwhile, perhaps, he could get on with what he had come to Trieste to do, which was to find out what had happened to Lomax.

First, though, there was a report to write.

It was some time later that he remembered the letter he had stuffed in his pocket. He took it out now and read it through properly.

It was indeed from Lomax's Auntie Vi and a reply to the letter he had sent. She thanked him for writing. A letter had arrived from the Foreign Office that very same morning, she said, but it was not the same thing. Somehow on a thing like this it helped to hear from someone personally. Seymour had mentioned the pleasure which Lomax seemed to have found in his new posting. She said that something of that pleasure had come through in his letters home.

She caught herself up. Well, she hoped it had been a home to him. He had come to them from Dublin as a boy of eleven when his mother, Auntie Vi's sister, had died. He had been a shy, odd little creature, she said, who had found it difficult to settle in. For a long time his only interest had been stamps. He had been quite bright, though, and had done well at school. They had been surprised all the same when he had chosen to apply for the Consular service; and even more surprised when he had been accepted. Perhaps it was the stamps that had put it into his mind. No one in their family, which was a decent, honest one, had ever done anything like that before. His mother, Auntie Vi said, would have been proud of him.

She said nothing about his father. He would have been Irish, perhaps? That might account for the Dublin. Died, possibly, like his wife? Or simply disappeared from the scene. Disappeared from Auntie Vi's scene, anyway.

She said that although they had not seen Lomax for some time, they would miss him. Not being blessed with a child of their own, they had always treated him as a son. He had in turn looked on them as his parents. He had written to them regularly from his various postings all over the world and had sent them little presents, souvenirs, really, which were all they would have of him now but which at least would be a constant reminder of him.

She thanked Seymour again for his kindness in writing and said that if he was ever near Warrington he should call in; although she imagined that was not very likely. She expected he was always, like Lomax, in some other part of the world.

Seymour had the sense of a decent family stricken. With his own acute sense of family, he could guess how they felt. He was glad he had written.

He thought over what she had said. So Lomax had originally come from Ireland. He wondered if that accounted for his friendship with James and his helping him

131

over the cinema business. Perhaps, too, it had stirred old loyalties and old attitudes, an old nationalism that went back to childhood, ever a romantic siding with the underdog which seemed suddenly relevant again when he came to Trieste.

There was a knocking on the door. Someone was trying to get in. He had forgotten he had locked it. He went to the door and opened it.

A man was standing there who seemed vaguely familiar. He clicked his heels.

'Rakic,' he said.

Seymour remembered him now. He was the man who had talked to Marinetti about hiring the Politeama for his Futurist Evening. Someone to do with Machnich.

'You are the Consul?' he said.

'No.'

The man corrected himself.

'Of course not. Lomax was the Consul. And Lomax is dead. But you . . .?' He seemed puzzled. 'I thought they said that you –'

'No,' said Seymour. 'I am just here temporarily. Passing through. I am a King's Messenger.

'King's . . .?'

'Messenger. I carry messages. Diplomatic ones.'

'Ah, yes, I see. And what, exactly, are you doing here?'

And what, exactly, business was it of his, thought Seymour, reacting to the tone?

'Carrying messages,' he said, however. 'I just happened to be here when Lomax was found.'

'Ah, yes. So you are nothing, then.'

'I wouldn't quite put it like that,' said Seymour.

The man seemed to realize how he sounded.

'I am sorry,' he said, though only half graciously. 'I meant, in the context of Trieste –'

'I am passing through,' said Seymour. 'And you?'

He had had enough of this boorish questioning.

'Machnich sent me.'

A little unwillingly, Seymour showed him in. They sat down in the inner office. Rakic looked around curiously at the walls.

'Decadent,' he pronounced.

'Out of the usual, definitely.'

Rakic shrugged. The pictures did not really interest him.

'You come from Machnich?'

'Yes.' Rakic studied him for a moment. 'He has heard about Koskash,' he said.

'Yes?'

'It is of concern to him. Will you tell me, please, what happened?'

Seymour hesitated. Why should he tell this man?

Rakic evidently guessed what he was thinking.

'Perhaps you do not know. Machnich is a Serb.'

'Koskash is not a Serb.'

Rakic made an impatient gesture with his hand.

'It was to do with Serbs. Did they not explain that to you?'

'Why should that matter to Machnich?'

'Because he is a Serb, as I say. He is a big man in Trieste. The biggest Serb. And so the other Serbs look to him. When something happens that affects Serbs, they turn to him. And so he needs to know what happened yesterday.'

Rather grudgingly, Seymour told him as much as he knew.

'The two who came and asked for papers, they were Schneider's men, yes?'

'Yes.'

'So Schneider knows.'

It was a statement rather than a question and did not need answering. Seymour had a question of his own.

'And Machnich knows, too, does he? About the escape route?'

Rakic did not answer him directly.

133

'Machnich looks after his own,' he said.

'The Consulate was being used illicitly,' said Seymour coldly.

Rakic gestured dismissal again.

'Lomax knew.'

He seemed to be thinking.

'You will be staying here?' he said. 'Until someone else comes out?'

'Probably.'

'Then you must go and see Koskash.'

'I may well go and see him.'

'See him. It is important. He is weak. His wife is strong, but he is weak. You must see him every day.'

Seymour made no reply.

'Every day!' insisted Rakic.

'Why is Machnich so concerned?' asked Seymour.

'As I told you, because this touches the Serbs.'

'Not because it might touch him?'

Rakic laughed.

'That, too, no doubt,' he said drily. It was the first time the obsessive single-mindedness had lifted. 'However,' he said, 'that is not his only concern. He looks after his own, as I have said. And Mrs Koskash is a Serb.'

He sat there looking at Seymour. He seemed to be weighing him up.

'She must not be left on her own,' he said.

Then he seemed to make up his mind. He stood up.

'Machnich wishes to see you,' he said. 'The Stella Polare at eleven. Tomorrow.'

Chapter Ten

There was a man waiting outside the Consulate the next morning when Seymour arrived. He turned round and smiled.

'Signor Seymour?'

'*Si.*'

He bowed, in a formal, old-fashioned way.

'Augstein. Mrs Koskash sent me. She thought I might be of use.'

He had, he said, been the Consulate's clerk before Koskash and had been retired for some years now.

'However,' he said cheerfully, 'I do not expect things to have changed much. You will need some temporary help, and it will not be like getting in someone completely new to the job.'

'Mrs Koskash sent you?'

'Yes. She said she owed you something,' said Augstein quietly.

He was an elderly, grey-haired man, stooping slightly but still alert and active. When Seymour took him into the Consulate he looked around fondly.

'Much the same,' he said.

He went to Koskash's desk. It was locked.

He went across to a shelf with a row of box files and felt between them.

'We used to leave the key here. Ah!'

He showed it to Seymour.

'As I said, I don't expect things have changed much. Mr Koskash is an orderly man and I, too, was orderly.'

135

He sat down at Koskash's desk and pulled the mail in the in-tray towards him. He glanced at some of the letters and then went to the files.

'Ah, yes,' he said, 'we are almost up to date. It will not take long to catch up. Mr Koskash is most conscientious.'

He took out some forms.

'They are just the same,' he said, with satisfaction.

He took up a pen and began to write.

Seymour hesitated. He could certainly do with the help. And yet he could not help feeling a little suspicious.

He went into the inner office, wavered and then came back.

'I would like,' he said, 'to consult the personnel files. The back files, please.'

'Certainly.'

Augstein rose from his desk and in a moment had laid two files on Seymour's desk.

It was as Augstein had said. He had indeed been Koskash's predecessor. He had worked in the Consulate for over thirty years, serving both of Lomax's predecessors. There were his original references and here was a testimonial written at the point when he was handing over. It was in glowing terms: 'thorough', 'conscientious', 'steady', 'reliable'. It was like an identikit version of Koskash.

And yet Koskash had turned out not to be entirely reliable, at least, not from the Consulate's point of view. And Seymour still had that *fait accompli* feeling. Perhaps there was nothing in it. Perhaps he was being too distrustful. Perhaps Mrs Koskash was merely trying to make amends.

He turned back through the old references. Then he closed the file and went in to Augstein.

'Everything seems to be as you said. I see you were indeed here before Koskash. And for a long time, too!'

'Too long, perhaps,' said Augstein, sighing. 'But jobs like this were not easy to get, not for people like me, anyway.'

'People like you?'

136

'New immigrants. I was new, thirty years ago,' he said, smiling.

'And where did you come from?'

'Belgrade.'

'Serbia?'

'Yes.'

'But an Austrian father? With that name?'

'Yes.' Augstein smiled again. 'Perhaps that is why they appointed me. It certainly made it easier in dealing with the authorities.'

Another Serb, thought Seymour. Perhaps that didn't matter. It was natural for people of a kind to stick together, he knew that from his own experience in the East End. It was perfectly reasonable that Mrs Koskash should send along someone she knew and that that person should be a Serb like her. Perhaps that was how Koskash had got the job in the first place. All the same, Seymour felt uneasy. He had the sense of a clan closing round him. Perhaps that was how it tended to be in the Balkans. An individual was never quite just an individual, as Maddalena had said. Perhaps that was the mistake Lomax had made. You helped an individual, or individuals, but you got drawn into a group; and where did the group's loyalties begin and end?

The Stella Polare was one of the old coffee houses of Trieste and as soon as Seymour went in he realized that up till now he had been missing something about Trieste. For this was the other side of Trieste, the part complementary to the tables in the outdoor cafés in the Piazza Grande, the Italian sparkle in the sunshine. If they were Italians, this was Austrian. Dark wood everywhere, low-beamed roofs, cosy corners. There were comfortable, horsehair-stuffed sofas in the recesses and newspapers on the tables. It was like the English Club but somehow heavier, solider, warmer. *Gemütlich*. The Austrian word popped up in his mind.

Drifting out of the kitchen came the smells of Middle Europe: of the spicy, dumplinged broths of Budapest, the breadcrumbed schnitzels of Vienna, of venison and boar from the Bohemian forests, of paprika and rye bread and apple. The smells stirred memories of home for Seymour; not just his own home but the homes he had gone into in the East End with old Appelmann, immigrants' homes still carrying with them culinary evidence of their roots.

At this hour, of course, the predominant smell was that of coffee and that seemed different, too, from the coffees of the piazza or of the Canal Grande. This was coffee with cream, the coffee of Vienna.

A man got up from a table in a corner and came towards him.

'Signor Seymour?'

'Signor Machnich?'

They shook hands. Machnich led him back to his table.

'You like the place, yes?'

'One of the old cafés,' said Seymour.

'Old, yes.' Machnich looked around with satisfaction. 'This is the real Trieste,' he said. 'Where the real business of the city gets done.'

Everyone here, and there were quite a few of them even this early in the morning, distributed about the recesses and corners, was wearing a suit. And a suit, not a uniform. This, he realized, was the commercial heart of the city: old, yes, as Machnich had said, older, perhaps, even than the uniforms.

'When I first came to Trieste,' said Machnich, 'I put my head in here and said: no, this is not the place for me. But then I was just a poor shopkeeper. Now I know that if I did not come here they would think I was still just a poor shopkeeper.' He shrugged. 'I do not really care what they think. But if they see me here, where there is money, they will think I have money, and money breeds money. There is another thing. You see all this?'

The sweep of his arm took in the solid tables and comfortable chairs and the heavy, opulent woodwork.

'It is sound. And the people here are sound, or like to think they are. They belong to the old Trieste. The Trieste of old, safe money. The Trieste that even Austrians respect. And while I am here people will think that I, too, am sound. There are times,' he said, 'when that can be an advantage.'

He sat back in his chair. He was a great bull of a man, with a thick, bull-like neck and alert unblinking eyes.

'Like now?' said Seymour.

Machnich looked at him sharply. Then his face creased up into a smile.

'Yes,' he agreed. 'Like now. But why do you say that?'

'I gather that you're worried about Koskash.'

'Not *about*,' said Machnich. '*For*. I am worried for Koskash. What they might do to him.'

'But why should you be worried about that?'

'I worry,' said Machnich, 'because he is one of mine.'

'He's not a Serb.'

'He counts as one. Married to one. The next best thing.' His face creased up again. 'Almost a Serb,' he said jovially. 'And so I look after him. Machnich looks after his own.'

Seymour shook his head.

'I don't think so,' he said.

The smile faded.

'What is this?' said Machnich.

'You may look after your own. But that is not why you are concerned about Koskash.'

'What is this you are saying?'

'I think you are concerned about Koskash because you are worried about what he might say. What he might tell the authorities.'

Machnich put a large forefinger on Seymour's chest.

'Me? Worried? Listen,' he said. 'Machnich has no worries. What do I care what he tells the authorities? I am in with the Austrians.' He looked around the café. 'That is what I have been telling you.'

139

'Yes, I know you have. But I still think you are worried about what Koskash might say.'

'What could Koskash say?'

The sharp eyes were watching him closely.

'He might tell them about your connection with the escape route.'

'Escape route? What escape route?'

'The escape route for Serbian students. Serbians. Your people. And Machnich looks after his own.'

'I know nothing about any escape route,' said Machnich flatly.

'No?'

'No!'

'Then why are you worried about what Koskash might say?'

The big neck became red.

'I am *not* worried about what Koskash might say.'

Seymour shrugged.

'What was it you wanted to see me about?' he said.

For a moment Machnich continued to look at him angrily. Then the red faded from his neck, his face relaxed and he gave a smile that was almost roguish.

'About Lomax,' he said.

He waved an arm and a waiter instantly brought coffee. Machnich waited while he poured it out. Then he looked at Seymour.

'Signor Lomax was different,' he said.

'Different?'

'Not like the usual consuls. Not like the usual officials here in Trieste. All just paper-pushers.' He snapped his fingers. 'Paper-pushers! I shit on them. But Signor Lomax was not like that. We were,' he said unexpectedly, 'people of the same type.'

'Really? In what respect?'

'Heart. We are people of heart. And so it hurt me,' he

said, 'here,' he put his hand on his heart, 'when I heard that he had gone.'

'You knew him well?'

'Well, yes. We had worked together.'

'Over the Irish cinemas?'

Machnich looked surprised.

'You know about that?'

'A little.'

'Finished,' said Machnich. 'Long ago. Concluded.'

'Satisfactorily, I hope?'

'No.'

'No?'

'No. I lost money.'

'Not because of Signor Lomax, I hope?'

'Signor Lomax? No. Nothing to do with him. My fault, mine.' He touched himself in the chest. 'I should never have gone in in the first place. I let myself be talked into it. By that crazy Irishman. But that was not Signor Lomax's fault. Mine!'

'What went wrong?'

'No one came.'

'I'm surprised at that. I remember going to the cinema in London –'

'London?' interrupted Machnich. 'Cinema? Where?'

'In the East End.'

'I don't know of one there.'

'It's not there. Not any more. It went bust.'

'There!' said Machnich gloomily. 'You see? Dublin, London – bust!' He shook his head. 'And you know why? New, too new for them. Those places are backward! Not like Trieste. In Trieste everyone goes to the cinema. Even those madmen who want to take over the Politeama next week for the night.'

'The Futurists?'

'Futurists, my ass! What do they know about the future? Listen, I'm the future, not those stupid bastards. Business is the future. Not art. That's what I told Signor Lomax.'

'And what did he say?'

141

'He said we ought to get together. Business and Art. And the cinema was where it could happen. "No thanks," I said. "I've had enough of artists. Look what one bloody artist has cost me!" Well, he laughed. "Better luck next time," he said. "Listen," I said. "There's not going to be a next time. In future, me and art are going to stay apart."'

'From the way you talk,' said Seymour, 'you got on well with Signor Lomax.'

'Well, I did. I found him . . . very sympathetic.'

'And not just over business.'

'Not just over business?'

'He helped you with the escape route, didn't he?'

Machnich looked at him shrewdly but did not reply. Then he said:

'Perhaps.'

'He came to see you on the night that he died,' said Seymour.

'Yes.'

'What did you talk about?'

'Business.'

'What business? Not the cinemas. You said yourself that was all over.'

'Not just business.'

'The escape route.'

'Perhaps.'

'What did you say about the escape route?'

Machnich shrugged. 'Perhaps that that was all over, too.'

'Was he saying that? Or were you?'

'Perhaps we both were. That it was time to stop.'

'You didn't disagree over that?'

'No. We thought alike. We always – nearly always – thought alike. As I say, we were people of the same type.' He laid his hand on his heart. 'People of heart. And yet at the same time,' he put a finger alongside his nose, 'people

142

of sense. Not airy-fairy. That is what I liked about Signor Lomax. Down to earth but good of heart. Like me.'

'So you talked,' said Seymour, 'and then he left. Do you know where for? Or what he was going to do?'

'No,' said Machnich. 'I only know what happened. He went out of the door and then – then I did not see him again. And in my heart there is a kind of absence.'

As Seymour went out, Machnich, who had accompanied him to the door, said:

'You will not forget to keep visiting Koskash, will you?'

Seymour wondered, as he walked away, if that had been the whole point of the invitation to the Stella Polare, to reinforce what Rakic had said. But Machnich had said he wanted to talk not about Koskash but about Lomax. What, though, had he said about Lomax? That, tacitly, he had known about (been involved with?) the escape route. But this Seymour had already known. Reinforcement, again? Or perhaps it had been something else: an offer to trade. You keep visiting Koskash, so that they won't beat the truth out of him, and I'll keep quiet about Lomax's involvement.

He was conscious, as he turned towards the Piazza Grande, of his 'shadow' slipping in behind him. He had come to take him for granted now, would almost miss him if he wasn't there. But he was always there. What sort of place was it where you became so accustomed to being followed that you felt uncomfortable if you weren't being? He shrugged his shoulders. Despite the sunshine there were shadows to Trieste, of all kinds.

Almost deliberately, almost, as it were, in defiance of Trilby, Seymour sat down with the artists. He sat next to Maddalena. As soon as he did so he realized how much he had been missing her. Her strong physical presence seemed suddenly to make him complete again. He almost

143

put out his hand and touched her but that would have been too obvious, give away too much, not least to the others. He could sense, though, that she felt the same. She hurried towards him eagerly. After a moment she put her hand on his hand.

There was activity in the piazza this morning. A procession was coming across towards them. It seemed to be an official one of some sort. First came the *lamparetti*, fiercely mustachioed and in Tyrolean hats. Then came the band, blowing and banging and in military step. Then came an open carriage containing two splendid figures, epauletted, braided and plumed. The Governor at least? But no. Behind the carriage was another one, in which sat a solitary figure even more heavily drenched in gilt and plumed in even brighter plumes.

And now they saw that a red carpet had been laid between the tables. The first carriage went past the end of the carpet and stopped. The two splendid figures descended and went to the end of the carpet to receive the second carriage. They opened its doors and the even more splendid figure stepped down on to the carpet, where, behind the first two splendid figures, a little group of men were waiting nervously to receive it. They, too, wore uniforms, equally gorgeous, but to the trained eye, they were as nothing.

For these were merely the officials of the Assicurazioni Generale, whose offices occupied the Palazzo Stratti above the Caffé degli Specchi, which the Governor was visiting that day to unveil a plaque. After much bowing and scraping and saluting they led him into the building. The band arranged itself on the steps of the entrance and began to play a military march. When it ended there was a polite ripple of applause from the people at the Caffé's tables.

'What's all this?' asked Maddalena.

'I think I read about it somewhere,' said Luigi. 'Isn't he unveiling a plaque?'

'Who to?'

144

'The Archduchess, I think.'

'What has *she* got to do with it?'

'Perhaps she has got shares in the Assicurazioni?' offered Lorenzo.

'I have got shares in the Assicurazioni,' said Alfredo, 'and no one is putting up a plaque to me!'

'You have got shares in the Assicurazioni, Alfredo?' said Maddalena, astonished.

'Yes. Two. My aunt left me them when she died.'

'Capitalist!'

The *lamparetti* had spread out along the edges of the carpet. One of them was just beside the artists. Maddalena looked up at him.

'What all this about a plaque?' she said.

'It's to commemorate the Assicurazioni's having been here for fifty years. Fifty years of service to Trieste!'

'Fifty years of ripping people off!'

'I'm sorry you see it that way.'

'What about the Archduchess?'

'The Archduchess?'

'I thought she was somehow involved.'

'Not as far as I know. It's just the Assicurazioni.'

'Anyway, I don't think the Governor should be doing this.'

'Oh? Why not?'

'He's only going there because it's big. He never goes to people like Simonetti, does he?'

'Simonetti?'

'The tobacconist at the corner. I'll bet he's been there for fifty years.'

'Well, hell –'

'Or Niccolo.'

'Niccolo?'

'The ice-cream seller. He looks very old.'

'Well, you can't go and see everybody!'

'You know why he's going to the Assicurazioni? It's because it's big. And because it backs the Austrians.'

'Young lady, I don't like your tone.'

145

'Shut up, Maddalena,' said Lorenzo nervously.

'If it backed irredentism, would he be going there?'

'Young woman, are you looking for trouble?'

Luigi intervened hastily.

'No, she's not,' he said. 'How could you think such a thing? She's looking for a waiter to bring us another drink, that's all. Aren't you, Maddalena?'

'Of course!' said Maddalena sweetly, and waved her arm vigorously.

A waiter, who had heard the whole exchange, came up, beaming.

'Something for the irredentists?' he said. 'What will you have?'

They were all at it, thought Seymour, all baiting the Austrians.

There was a little silence.

Then Lorenzo said to Luigi:

'Actually, it's not the Assicurazioni that I mind, it's the music.'

'Terrible, isn't it?'

'Do you think they select them on the basis of their tin ears?'

'No, I think they're probably all right when they start. It's just the training that they're given.

'When they go into the army, you mean?'

'Yes. It makes them sort of deaf.'

'Well, I think you need to be if you're working for the government in Trieste.'

'Listen –' began the policeman.

'Yes, officer?' said Luigi innocently.

'I don't like that kind of talk.'

'Oh, but we're only talking about music. I'd be interested to hear your views. What's your opinion of Lehar?'

'Or Verdi?' said Lorenzo.

'Or Rossini,' said Alfredo swiftly. 'Personally, I think . . .' And he moved the conversation deftly, and unequivocally, on to musical grounds.

*   *   *

Koskash was sitting on a bed. He jumped up when he saw Seymour, put his heels together and bowed formally.

'I wish to apologize,' he said. 'I know I have not behaved correctly. I am very sorry.'

Seymour asked how he had been treated.

'I am well, thank you,' said Koskash.

There were no signs of ill-usage.

Seymour went to the spy-hole and checked. There was no one listening outside. They were playing fair. Or perhaps they weren't bothered. He went back to Koskash.

'Koskash,' he said, 'I shall come regularly. You understand?'

Koskash nodded.

'I think I do,' he said. 'And thank you.'

'There are people outside who are concerned for you. Your wife.' Koskash looked troubled and seemed about to say something but then didn't. 'And others.' Koskash nodded. 'These others are, I think, worried about what you might say.'

'They need not be,' said Koskash. 'I shall say nothing.'

'That may not be a good idea. And it may be unnecessary. They know quite a lot already. The men who came to you were policemen, planted to trap you. You could tell them some things. It might make it easier for you. This is just advice, meant to help you.'

Koskash nodded.

'Thank you,' he said. 'I understand.'

'You need not tell them everything, of course. That is up to you. But I would be grateful if you could tell *me* something.'

'If I can help,' said Koskash, 'I would wish to. I owe it.'

'It is about Machnich. And about Lomax. I gather that they got on well?'

Koskash nodded.

'Surprisingly well. For two men so different. I think it began when they met over the cinema business. They hit it off and then they began to meet socially. Not all the time but quite often. Usually it was at the Stella Polare but

147

sometimes Machnich came here.' Koskash caught himself. 'That is, to the Consulate. I would take in coffee and they would be chatting away like old friends. But then something happened, I don't know what, and Machnich didn't come any more. Instead he sent Rakic. You know Rakic? Well, he is very different and I don't think Signor Lomax liked him. But perhaps that was why Machnich sent him – to show Signor Lomax that they weren't friends any more.'

'There must have been some reason for sending him. Other than that, I mean. Some business reason or work reason.'

'If there was, I do not know it. But suddenly Rakic was here all the time, every day. And Signor Lomax grew more and more unhappy.'

Seymour heard footsteps in the corridor outside coming towards the cell. He stood up.

'Thank you, Koskash,' he said. 'That was most helpful.'

Koskash accompanied him to the door. Just before it opened, he said:

'Tell my wife that I am well. And that – that she mustn't do anything. I am afraid that she may blame herself and go to the police. Tell her not to. Tell her it will be easier for me if I know that she is outside. That I can bear it. And that she is not to do anything foolish. She must think of herself, only of herself, and not of me.'

Maddalena called in at the Consulate that evening. Seymour had invited her out to dinner and they had arranged that she should pick him up. She came into the inner room, Lomax's room, and glanced at the pictures.

'He was never really sure about them,' she said. 'Sometimes he liked them, and said that they were bold and refreshing and new. And sometimes he said that they showed everything falling apart and that that was bad, the world wasn't like that. It wasn't *that* bad.'

She went up to one of the pictures.

'But the wheel *is* coming off,' she said. 'And that means the car is going to crash, doesn't it? He was right about that.'

She sat down in one of the chairs.

'You have come here to find out about Lomax, haven't you? I don't believe you are a Messenger at all. I think you may be a policeman.' She shrugged. 'I don't care if you are. Not if you're here to find out what happened to Lomax.'

Seymour said nothing.

'I have done what you asked,' she said. 'I have talked to the students. I asked them if any of them had tried to go to the reception at the Casa Revoltella, had asked Lomax to take them. But they said not. And they said that they wouldn't have caused trouble at the reception, not just at the moment, anyway, because the Governor would be there and he had it in enough for students as it was, what with all this Bosnian business.'

'You know that Lomax was helping Serbian students to get out of Trieste? Or at any rate going along with it.'

Maddalena nodded.

'That is what the students say. They think that may have been why the Austrians killed him.'

'The *Austrians* killed him?' said Seymour incredulously.

'That is what they say. But then students always say such wild things.'

As they were going out, she looked at the pictures again.

'He spoke about these the last time I saw him. It was just before he died. He said that sometimes artists saw things that other people didn't. About the world, I mean.'

'People always think that the wheels are coming off the world.'

'I know. And Lomax said that diplomats were worse than anybody at thinking that. That they always thought they were sitting on a powder-bag which was about to explode. But that sometimes they were right.'

149

Chapter Eleven

In one of the streets leading to the Piazza Grande there were some large poster hoardings. Usually they displayed advertisements for local shops or even for the cinema. Whatever they were displaying today was unusually arresting, for a large knot of people was gathered in front of them.

Seymour, taller than most Triestians, was able to see over the heads. He read:

Futurist Evening. The Politeama on Saturday.

Underneath, it said:

Art Breaks into the Future! Art IS the Future!

Beneath that were two separate posters, alongside each other. One said:

The Future is Here! At the Politeama on Saturday. Embrace it!

Scribbled beneath *that* were the words:

And your Girl Friend!

And then another, different, scribble:

But not too closely! Otherwise you'll have to pay for the infant.

The poster next to it showed a caricature reproduction of the Mona Lisa. The corners of her mouth were exaggerated into a depressed droop. *Art is Tired!* read the caption. Underneath, the scribble, which Seymour now saw as part of the poster, said:

No, it's not! All she needs is a Man!

Another artist had added a bristly moustache to the face and then:

She IS a Man!

Just along the street was another poster which at first seemed to consist of the single word, written huge:
SMASH
But, then, down the edge, much smaller, one saw a column of other words:
Galleries
Museums
Libraries
Police Stations
The Assicurazioni Generale
and then, right at the end:
The Hapsburgs
Get rid of the Old, ran a caption around the bottom, *Let in the New. Let Art let in the Future!*
A man detached himself from the group of viewers.
'Children!' he said, with a sneer.
It was Rakic.
'What rubbish!' he said, seeing Seymour and half-recognizing him. 'To think people are being invited to an evening of that!'
Now he did recognize Seymour.
'The King's Messenger? Yes?'
'Yes.'
'And you carry messages, you said. Yes?'
'Yes. For the Foreign Office in London. To consulates and embassies.'
'And back again?'
'Sometimes, yes.'
Rakic smiled.
'And what message will you be carrying back to London from Trieste? Not about this, I hope,' he said, gesturing towards the posters.
'No. I don't think so. Only messages of diplomatic significance.'
'And this is not,' said Rakic, somehow with satisfaction. 'It is childish rubbish. And yet people will be going to their Evening! Important people. The Governor!' He shook his head in wonderment.
'These are just advertisements,' said Seymour, moved,

for some reason, to speak up on behalf of Marinetti. 'There may be more to the Evening than this.'

Rakic seemed struck.

'More to the Evening? Well, perhaps you are right. We must hope so. For the sake of the people who are going. The important people.' He shrugged. 'Well, it is no concern of mine. So long as the money for the hall has been paid.'

Seymour had not heard from Kornbluth for two or three days, despite his promise to keep him informed. Two or three days were perhaps not much. All the same . . .

He made up his mind to see Kornbluth and later in the morning called in on him at the police station. Kornbluth was back to his most stolid and looked up at Seymour with none of his usual affability.

'I was wondering how you were getting on,' said Seymour.

Kornbluth, almost reluctantly, gestured to him to sit down.

'Badly,' he said. 'There have been no further developments.'

'You have found no one who saw Lomax after he had left the cinema that night?'

'We have asked,' said Kornbluth, 'but no one seems to have seen him.'

'Have you been asking about the right time?' said Seymour.

'The right time?'

'Not when the performance ended. Later.'

'Later?'

'He went back into the cinema. To see Machnich. He would have left later than we thought.'

'Did he, now?'

Kornbluth sat there thinking.

'How do you know?' he asked.

'Someone told me. And I have spoken to Machnich.'

Kornbluth thought some more.

152

'You will check?' Seymour pressed him. 'For the new time?'

'Yes.'

Seymour sensed reluctance, however.

'Is anything wrong? Something gone wrong with the investigation? Have I done something?'

'No, no,' said Kornbluth hurriedly. 'All is as it should be.' He paused. 'It is just that – well, we have been told to hold back a little on the investigation.'

'Hold back? Who by?'

'I am afraid I cannot say,' said Kornbluth unhappily.

'Schneider? But, Christ –'

'Listen,' said Kornbluth. 'I am sorry. It is not as I would have it. But sometimes it is necessary to hold back on one thing so that you can progress on another.'

'But he *has* progressed on another! He got Koskash. He's closed that escape route down. You mean to say there's something *else*? Somebody *else* to do with Lomax?'

Kornbluth put up a hand.

'I say nothing,' he said. 'I know nothing. That is because I *would* know nothing. Schneider doesn't tell me what he's doing. All I know is that he's asked me to hold back.'

'But do you have to? I mean, if you've got an investigation going –'

'If Schneider asks,' said Kornbluth, 'I have to. Look, I don't like it. Those bastards over there get up my nose. I'm an ordinary policeman, right? And I like to get on with my ordinary work in an ordinary way. And I don't like those bastards coming in over my head and ordering me around. But I've got to put up with it, see? Schneider's a bloody General and I'm a bloody Inspector, and what his lot says, goes, and what my lot says, doesn't. So there you have it. If I could do something about it, I would. If I could put one across him, I would. But I can't. I'll do what I can for you. I'll check possible witnesses at the new time. But don't expect too much, that's all. Schneider's got his heel on me, the same as he has on everyone else.'

* * *

153

Seymour walked away simmering. He wondered, as he walked, and as his 'shadow' fell in behind him, whether he should write a letter of protest to the people back in the Foreign Office and savoured, for a moment, a few juicy phrases that he could put in. But then a note of caution crept in. This was probably happening to diplomats all the time. Governments were probably always saying something or doing something to them and they just had to swallow it. They couldn't answer back and it wouldn't be much good writing complaining letters to London. He could just imagine that supercilious bastard back in London getting a letter from him. 'Always knew he wasn't up to it,' he could hear him saying. 'From the East End. Not a diplomat, of course.'

But there was another reason why perhaps it would be best not to write. At least, not yet. Schneider evidently thought there was something else he had to find out. Something else, probably about Lomax, something more than just involvement in the escape route. It would be better if Seymour could discover what that was before writing any complaining letters. Because Schneider might, just might, be in the right.

He turned up an alleyway and heard Trilby's footsteps echoing behind him. That was another thing he felt like complaining about. It was almost like cheek. Of course, Schneider didn't know, not for sure, that he was a policeman, but even if he had been a diplomat . . .

A consul like Lomax. Had Lomax been followed, too? Because if he had . . .

Seymour turned on his heel, throwing Trilby into confusion, and walked back the way he had come. A few moments later he was being shown into Schneider's office.

Schneider looked up, smiling politely.

'Still here, then?'

'Still here,' said Seymour, 'and still hoping to find out what happened to Lomax.'

'You'd better ask Kornbluth –'

154

'Not much point in doing that,' said Seymour, 'is it?'
The smile faded.

'What is it that you are meaning?' said Schneider.

'Not much point in doing that when you're the one I should be approaching.'

'Mr Kornbluth is the officer –' began Schneider, and then stopped.

'You are the one who is holding all the loose ends,' said Seymour. 'I want to know about the pattern.'

Schneider said nothing for a moment, then sighed.

'You know about the pattern. Or as much about it as I do. I told you. I suspect his involvement with the Serbs. I suspect there was more to it than just helping students to escape. If I am right, it is you that should be doing the explaining.'

'Lomax was killed,' said Seymour, 'and I want to know who killed him.'

'So do I,' said Schneider. 'Of course. And if you ask Mr Kornbluth –'

'You know more than Kornbluth. You knew more right from the start. Because you were having him followed. You knew, for instance, but did not tell Kornbluth, that after leaving the Piazza Grande and the artists he went to the Edison cinema. You knew that after the performance, after saying goodbye to James Juice he went back in. You would have worked out that he went to see Machnich.'

'Well?'

'Well? You tell me.'

Schneider looked at him for a moment.

'What do you want to know?' he said quietly.

'What I want to know is what happened when he came out. The second time. Your man was there. What did he see?'

Schneider thought, then sighed again.

'Nothing,' he said.

'Nothing?'

'He did not come out.'

'But then –'

'Unless he came out by some other door. We have, of

course, spoken to Machnich. He swears that after their conversation, Lomax left. There are two cleaners there who support that. One never believes entirely but I think they were speaking the truth.'

'He left, but your man did not see him?'

Schneider nodded.

'That is what Machnich says must have happened. Unfortunately, he could be right. My men are not what they ought to be.'

'You shadow me, too,' said Seymour.

'That is for your own protection.'

Seymour hoped that if that was so, and he very much doubted it, then whoever was shadowing him would show rather more efficiency than the man who had been shadowing Lomax.

Mrs Koskash was waiting for him at the Consulate.

'You have been to see him?'

'Yes. He is well. As well as can be expected. They have not touched him yet.'

'Keep going,' said Mrs Koskash. 'Go to see him every day.'

'He asked me to pass a message to you. It was that you shouldn't do anything – anything precipitate. Like turning yourself in. He said that it would be easier for him if he knew that you were outside.'

'The fool!' said Mrs Koskash. The hard shell cracked, however. 'The fool!' she said again, softly.

Augstein came in with two cups of coffee.

'Thank you for sending him,' said Seymour, when he had gone.

'It was the least we could do. Koskash was particularly anxious that the work of the Consulate should not suffer. More than it had to.'

'Augstein is a Serb, isn't he?'

She looked at him quickly.

'Does that worry you?'

'It didn't worry Lomax's predecessors.'

'He is a good, conscientious man.'

'It didn't worry Lomax's predecessors; but I wonder if it ought to worry me.'

'Because of what we did for the students, you mean? He had nothing to do with that. It happened after his time.'

'When did it start?'

'Two years ago. After the Austrians annexed Bosnia. There was protest and the Austrians cracked down. Mostly it was the young, students. Suddenly there were a lot of them trying to flee from the police. We felt we had to do something.'

'We?'

'The Serbs here. But I never intended it to become what it did. I thought I would do it once or twice only. And Koskash was happy with that. But when it grew, he was less happy. And I was less happy, not because it was dangerous, but because it wasn't fair, to him. But Machnich kept sending us more people. They all went to him because he is the Big Man, here, the big Serbian man, at any rate. And I think – I think he revelled in it. He thought of himself as the Saviour of his people. Machnich looks after his own, you know!

'But I think we would have stopped, anyway. It came to a head when he started sending us people who were not Serbs, not even students! I remember, he sent us two Herzegovinians. Herzegovinians! Look, I said, they're not Serbs. They're not even students. They're a pair of roughs, they look criminals to me. Just this once, he said. A special favour! I don't like the look of them, I said. Who knows what they might have done? They haven't done anything, he said. They're students, staying in the student hostel. But I wouldn't do it. I said, no, that's enough. And that man of his became very hot under the collar, but I stuck to it. No, I said, we've done enough. But then, of course, Machnich sent us some more. Proper students this time, so, well . . . It was a mistake. I should have stopped. For Koskash's sake.'

'When was this?' asked Seymour. 'When was it that the two Herzegovinians came along?'

157

'I can place it exactly. It was after Machnich started sending Rakic. There was a period when he seemed to be coming all the time. Koskash noticed it because Lomax became increasingly angry. But still he kept coming. Koskash thought he was badgering Lomax over something. Well, it was after that. Something happened, and then Rakic didn't want to see Lomax any more. But suddenly he wanted to see Koskash. It was about those Herzegovinians. Machnich came too and they were both very angry when he refused.'

Herzegovinians now, thought Seymour, after she had gone. Where the hell was Herzegovina? It must be another of those Balkan countries. And how exactly was Herzegovina aligned in all these disputes that seemed to occur in that part of the world? And did it matter? Not to anyone outside the Balkans and not, hitherto, to him. But maybe he should look into it when he got home. Do a bit of reading. It was shocking to be so ignorant. Especially when his own people, his mother, at least, came from that area.

And that was another thing. Nationalism. Half the trouble seemed to be that they all wanted to be independent, run their own show. Well, why not? A nuisance to everyone else, maybe, but why couldn't you just leave them to get on with it? He was certain about one thing, though: how right his family had been to get out of it!

He was still thinking about it when Maddalena arrived. She was another, caught up in all these local politics. Or at any rate, the local passions about politics, and there seemed to be plenty of those. Maddalena was certainly passionate, in all senses, but at least her political action was confined to daubing statues and making musical gibes at authority.

And much the same seemed to be true of that bunch of artists he had met in the Piazza Grande. They were Italians and seemed to want independence, or, at least, union with Italy – irredentism, was it? – as passionately as everyone

158

here seemed to want something else, but on the whole they stuck to their art, and that was harmless, surely?

Maybe that was why Lomax had turned to them – as a relief after having to do with everyone else! The Serbs, for instance. Clearly, he had felt a lot of sympathy for them, too much, probably, and that might have led him to go too far. But maybe he had felt that, as the Koskashes seemed to have done, and had tried to draw back, back to the sunshine of the piazza and the great ships in the bay, back to the inconsequential chatter and the pictures on the wall?

Maddalena had news for him.

'I think you've made a mistake,' she said. 'You've been thinking that Lomax did not go to that reception at the Casa Revoltella. But it seemed that he did.'

She said that she had been talking to some students and that two of them made some money in their spare time by working as waiters at wedding party receptions and the like. They had done some waiting at the reception at the Casa Revoltella, going round with trays of drinks and tit-bits. At one point, when things had slackened off, they had gone outside for a breath of fresh air. They had stood just outside the door, at the top of the steps, and looked down and had seen some men arguing. One of the men was trying to get in and another was trying to stop him. They were pretty sure that the second man had been Lomax.

In the end someone had summoned the major-domo and he had come down and ordered the first man away. And then, they thought, Lomax had mounted the stairs and gone in.

'What about the second man?' said Seymour. 'Did they know him?'

Maddalena said that they didn't, but that they didn't think he was a student. More like a soldier, one of them said, all stiff and upright. Not like an ordinary soldier, the other had corrected him: like an officer. Bossy, commanding.

'Commanding Lomax?' said Seymour.

'He tried to push past him,' said Maddalena, 'but Lomax wouldn't let him. He wouldn't be bossed.'

Seymour asked Augstein to find out from the Casa Revoltella who had been the major-domo on that occasion. Augstein, who seemed to know everybody in Trieste, didn't need to find out.

'Oh, that would have been Ravanelli,' he said.

He even told Seymour where he could find him: working at one of the big hotels.

Seymour went there.

Oh, yes, said Ravanelli, he had been there on that occasion. It was a big occasion and they had needed a big major-domo. It was pretty clear that Ravanelli thought he fitted that description. But it was a big occasion. Practically the whole of the Chamber of Commerce had been there, the Corps Diplomatique, such as it was in Trieste, had been there. Signor Barton had been there, from the English Club –

'Signor Machnich?' asked Seymour.

Well no, perhaps surprisingly since he usually reckoned to be at events like that if the Governor was going to be there. The Governor was there, with his wife. They came late but then, of course, you would expect that with important people –

'And Signor Lomax?'

'No.'

'No? But I thought . . .? Was there not some fracas at the bottom of the steps?'

Well, yes, there was, said Ravanelli, with an expression indicating distaste. A man had been trying to get in. Without an invitation. Well, there were always people like that. Fortunately Signor Lomax had spotted him and intercepted him. He seemed to know the man and had argued with him. Vehemently. The man had argued back and had tried to push past him but Signor Lomax had hung on. Someone had already gone for him, Ravanelli, though, and at that moment he had come down the steps. He had ordered the man to leave at once and the man had, of course, obeyed him; or, perhaps, it was the sight of the *lamparetti* coming out of the door.

There are times, said Seymour, when one has to speak with authority.

Well, there you are, said Ravanelli deprecatingly. He had to admit he had a certain presence. But what extraordinary behaviour! said Seymour. Surely the man must have seen this was an occasion of no ordinary significance. A reception at which the Governor himself was present was hardly the place for ordinary riff-raff.

Well, he wasn't exactly riff-raff –

Really? Then that made it worse. He must certainly have been off his head.

'Or Bosnian,' said Ravanelli, whose name was Italian and accent Triestino. 'An uncouth fellow, certainly.'

Had Signor Ravanelli informed the police?

Yes, but he had gone by the time they arrived; as was usually the case in Trieste.

But had Signor Ravanelli been able to give them a description of him? He was sure he had. A man like Signor Ravanelli, experienced, noticing. A good description, he would bet.

Well . . . It had all happened so quickly. But, as the Signor had said, he was a noticing man and he thought he had been able to supply something helpful to the police. After all, they didn't want this kind of thing happening too often . . .

Description, though, was always difficult, said Seymour. Signor Ravanelli had perceptively seen that the man was not riff-raff. But then how did you distinguish him from all the other men who were not riff-raff? Clothes? Face? Bearing?

He was well set up. Almost, well, military. In his bearing. And his voice, too.

A Colonel?

No, no, not a Colonel. A Captain, more like. Younger than a Colonel would be. And without quite the same

161

authority. The Signor would know. Asserting authority but not quite possessing it.

Seymour remarked again on how perceptive Signor Ravanelli was, and how fortunate it had been that he had been summoned in time to prevent the incident from developing into something worse.

'And then, you say, Signor Lomax did *not*, in fact, go in?'

Perhaps he had been too distressed by the incident. He was, perhaps, not as used to such things as he, Signor Ravanelli, was. But, no. He had waited, and seen the man go, and then had left himself.

Strange people had begun to appear in the Piazza Grande. They were dressed differently from the other people, more casually, even messily, and stood out strikingly from the usual close-cropped, uniformed male citizenry. They sat at the cafés' tables drinking and arguing.

The focus of their argument appeared to be a sheet of paper which many of them were carrying. Seymour managed to get a glimpse of it as he went past one of the tables. *Futurist Manifesto* was the heading, and *Citizens of the Future* . . . it began.

By the evening the piazza seemed full of Citizens of the Future. Seymour had had doubts about whether Marinetti's 'Futurist Evening', whatever that was, would get off the ground. He seemed to have been wrong.

Later in the evening he went through the piazza again. The arguing was still continuing. Indeed, it had grown more animated.

Marinetti himself was at one of the tables, not the artists' table this time.

'Art feels out the Future,' Seymour heard him declaiming. 'Art *is* the Future.'

But then there came a dissenting voice.

'No, it's not,' someone said.

'Not?' said Marinetti, caught, for the moment, off-balance.

'Art,' said the dissenting voice firmly, 'is outside time.'

162

Seymour recognized the voice now. It belonged to James.

Marinetti regathered himself.

'Futurist Art is the Future,' he roared. 'All other art belongs to the past.'

James aimed a blow at him, missed, and fell across the table.

'Other art,' bellowed Marinetti, 'the art of the museums, the galleries, the studios, is dead! It speaks in whispers. Polite, decorous whispers. "Oh, do please come and look at my beautiful, boring trees and my sweet, so sweet flowers! My beautiful blue waves –" Blue! Why should waves be blue, tell me that? Blue whispers, sends you to sleep. Why shouldn't waves be red?

'Close your eyes, and what colour do you see? Close them tighter, hold them shut. Red! Red, that is what you see. Red, that is what man brings to the world. Behind his polite, smiling eyes he sees the world as red.

'Not blue. Pooh, blue! Decorous, tame blue, decorous tame green. The decorous blues and greens, which were browns, the brown of the studios and the museums. Tame colours, tamed man.

'But Futurist Art is not tamed! It does not speak in whispers. It shouts!'

Which certainly seemed to be true, thought Seymour, if Marinetti himself was anything to go by.

'It cannot be ignored. You cannot walk by it. It explodes upon you!

'And it will release. It will release the energy that lies trapped behind these cold Austrian facades.

'It is the art of the cinema, not the art of the museum. It is the art of the Future and not of the past. It is the art of protest. And it will ignite. Futurist Art will ignite!'

James picked himself up off the table and hurled himself upon Marinetti. But now it was a friendly, approving, supporting embrace. The two danced off together among the tables to the enthusiastic cheers of the Citizens of the Future.

163

Chapter Twelve

Seymour was getting a taste for Trieste. When he walked down to the Consulate from his hotel in the morning, he liked to take in the Canal Grande, with its little working boats and the men loading and unloading – all small stuff, but, as Kornbluth had said on the first occasion when he had come here, somehow satisfyingly real, the tavernas up the side streets and the little cafés on the quays, the sea-gulls pecking for droppings, and the women at the end of the canal, sitting on the steps of the church, sewing.

This morning, as he walked along by the side of the canal, he was surprised to see the trim figure of Rakic. He was standing on the edge of the quay looking down into one of the boats and talking to its captain. Seymour had no particular urge to talk to Rakic and walked on past. His ear, registering language as always, picked up their speech, noticing it especially, perhaps, because it was in a language unfamiliar to him. Not quite unfamiliar, though, because he could work out what they were saying.

'Two days,' the captain said. 'That's all. We'll make Sarajevo in two days.'

The name of the place gave him a clue. Bosnian, that was it, that must be the language: close to Serbian.

'All right, then,' Rakic said. 'Be ready.'

He turned and saw Seymour.

'Ah, Signor Seymour!'

Seymour stopped unwillingly. Rakic hurried across.

'You are taking an early morning walk? Good for the digestion.'

'I'm staying at a hotel,' said Seymour. 'This is on my way to the Consulate.'

'Ah, yes.'

Rakic fell in alongside him.

'You are thinking about the message you will be taking back to London, perhaps? To the King?'

'Not much thought needed, I would say.'

'You will be telling him about Signor Lomax?'

'I think they already know.'

'Of course. And what,' he said, after a moment, 'was their reaction? When they heard?'

'I think they are waiting to hear more.'

'Of course. That is natural. It is natural for diplomats to react with caution. But what about the British Government? When all there is to be known, is known, how will it respond, do you think? With anger, that its Consul should be killed?'

'They regret Lomax's death, of course –'

Rakic interrupted him.

'But will they be angry? With the Austrians, for letting this happen?'

'Well, I don't know that it will be quite a question of that –'

'He is too small? A consul is, after all, a small thing. To a country like Britain, which has many consuls. And a consul in Trieste! What is Trieste to London? What is the death of the Consul in Trieste? Nothing! It is insignificant, the death of a fly. Or, perhaps, of a mosquito.'

Rakic seemed amused by the thought.

'Yes, a mosquito,' he repeated, with satisfaction. 'Always buzzing around, irritating, being difficult.'

'You found him difficult?'

Rakic gave him a weighing look.

'Yes, difficult,' he said.

'Others found him easy to get on with.'

'I found him difficult. You would think he was agreeing with you, going along with you. And then he would dig his heels in!'

165

'I'm sorry you found that.'

'Ah, well, it is not important. And a consul, you are right, is not important. His death does not make a big splash. I just wondered, that is all. Wondered if it would be enough to make England respond. But no, you are right. Too small.'

He was silent for a moment.

'But Austria, now, or Russia. How would they respond? If their man on the spot was killed? I think they might respond differently. The British Empire is so big, you see, and . . . complacent. It can afford to ignore such things. But the Austrian Empire is . . . touchy. It feels more threatened. It would not ignore something like that. No,' he said, shaking his head, 'it would not, could not, ignore a thing like that.'

Seymour went to see Koskash. He was pleased to see him.

'No,' he said, 'it is not that they have – No, it is just that one sits here alone for hour after hour so that it is nice to have someone to talk to.'

He looked at Seymour diffidently.

'While I have been here, I have been thinking. I have been thinking especially about the questions you asked. About Machnich and Signor Lomax. And I know that why you asked them is because you want to know why it was and how it was that Signor Lomax died. You are asking if it was connected with . . . with what I was doing. And as I sit here I have been asking myself the same question. I ask myself, could I have contributed, in any way, to his death?

'But I do not see how I could have done. I do not see how it could have been as you suppose. Machnich is not like that. He shouts and blusters but in the end he does not strike. In the end he is, actually, a coward. He does not like to confront people. He even had a secret door put in –'

'Yes,' said Seymour, 'I heard that.'

166

'– so that he could avoid people if necessary. If they were waiting for him outside the cinema. As sometimes they were.'

'The picket line –' said Seymour.

'There were always picket lines with Machnich,' said Koskash. 'It was not that he was especially hard, it was that he would get into a position and then be unable to climb down. My wife used to say that he was a fool. He would get into a conflict when it wasn't really necessary. And then he would stand on his dignity and it would be very hard to get him out of it.

'So, stupid and obstinate, yes – a typical Trieste bourgeois businessman, in fact – but not . . . not someone who would kill. I do not see how he could have done what you are supposing.'

'So,' said Mrs Koskash, 'you saw him?'

'Yes.'

'How was he?'

'He had been thinking.'

Mrs Koskash got up and began to pace about the room.

'That is bad,' she said. 'If he thinks, he will brood: and that will be bad for him.'

She was silent for a moment. Then –

'I do not think I can leave him there,' she said.

'I am not sure that even if you went to the police and gave yourself up, that would get him out,' said Seymour, guessing what she was thinking of doing. 'He has committed a crime and they will see it like that.'

'It is hard,' said Mrs Koskash, 'and gets harder every day.' She came back to the chair and sat down. 'What did you talk about?'

'I had asked him some questions, and he had been thinking about them.'

'What were the questions?'

167

'About Machnich and Lomax. They were, essentially,' he said, 'the questions I asked you.'

'And what did he say?'

'He knew why I was asking them; and said that Machnich was not that kind of man.'

Mrs Koskash nodded.

'Too weak,' she said. 'He liked everyone to think he was strong. The Big Man. He liked everyone to think that. Not just here but back where he came from. Perhaps that was even more important. He always had to justify himself in their eyes. Make them think that Machnich, the little boy from round the block, had made good. But, underneath, he was still just a little boy.

'However, they believed him. When they came to Trieste, they would go to him, thinking that he would be able to fix things for them.'

'Serbs?'

'Not always. Mostly, yes. But sometimes others, who had been to Belgrade and heard that he was the man in Trieste to go to.'

'Rakic?'

'Perhaps. I do not know otherwise what he is doing here. Or why he should have attached himself to Machnich.'

'You told me that there was a time when he was acting as go-between. Between Machnich and Lomax. You said that he seemed to be coming all the time.'

'Yes, that is right.'

'And then he stopped. And that was the moment when he started pressing Koskash over the two Herzegovinians.'

'Yes.'

'Could you tell me when that was? Exactly.'

'Well . . .'

'Was it, for instance, before the reception at the Casa Revoltella – you remember the reception? – or after?'

'He was definitely badgering Signor Lomax before. But the Herzegovinians – I think that was after.'

*　　*　　*

'Herzegovina?' said the newspaper seller. 'Don't get me started! Look, where do they stand? With us, or with the Bosnians? With the Bosnians. Well, that's asking for it, isn't it? All right, they've been with them for a long time. A few centuries. But what are a few centuries in the Balkans? Long enough to learn better. You would have thought.'

'Where exactly *is* Herzegovina?' said Seymour.

'You don't know? You really don't know? Christ, what do they teach you in schools in England! Look, you know where Bosnia is? Don't you?'

'Roughly,' said Seymour. 'Very roughly.'

'Go across the sea from the north of Italy and you'll hit it. Roughly. Well, Herzegovina is sort of mixed in with Bosnia. Not clear? Well, it's not really clear to the Herzegovinians themselves. And that's part of the trouble. They never know where they stand. And nor do you.'

'Well, no.'

'I think of them as being part of Bosnia. So if Bosnia doesn't like being taken over by Austria, they don't like it, either. Of course, there are not many of them, not as many as there are of the Bosnians, so in a way they don't matter much. But in my experience they're always causing difficulty out of proportion to their numbers. We've had a couple of them lately, throwing their weight around.

'Or, rather, we thought they were going to throw their weight around. We thought that bastard Machnich had brought them over to break the strike.'

'Break the strike? Blacklegs, you mean? You'd want more than two of them to do that.'

'Yes, I know. No, we thought he'd brought in a bit of muscle for the occasion. But actually it wasn't that. He didn't bring them in until we threatened to duff up that sidekick of his.'

'Rakic?'

'Yes, Rakic. You know Rakic? Well, so do we. Machnich sent him to talk to us about going back to work. Talk to us?' He laughed. 'Order us, more likely. That's what it turned out to be. I've met his sort before. In the army!

169

"Here are your orders, my men. Now bloody get on with it."

'Well, of course, he got nowhere. "Go and stuff yourself up your Bosnian backside," we said. And he got shirty. "You men need to watch out," he said. Well, he took us seriously, or, at least, Machnich did, and brought in those two Herzegovinian apes to act as bodyguard.'

'When was this?'

'I've been telling you! When we threatened to duff him up.'

'Yes, but when was that?'

'During the strike, of course.'

'Yes, but at what point during the strike? Was it – look, you know that big reception they had at the Casa Revoltella? For the Governor and such? Was it before that?'

'No.'

'No?'

'No. After. I remember that because it was just about that time that Mrs Koskash – she's our chairman, you know – said we should start thinking about negotiating a settlement. I remember it clearly because there was a lot of argument about it. "We don't want a negotiated settlement," some people said. "We want the bastard to give in." But she said no, and tried to arrange a meeting with Machnich. But he said he wouldn't, he had this big reception on, and he sent Rakic along instead. And that was when we threatened to duff him up.'

Lately, Seymour had been thinking about his family. In particular, he had been thinking about his mother, which was not a thing the macho policemen of the novels usually did. He had been thinking about her because she came from Vojvodina. 'Vojvodina?' his grandfather would sometimes tease his mother. 'Where the hell's that?' It was, in fact, at the top right-hand corner of Bosnia, lying immediately above Serbia, another of those Balkan countries

170

which any reasonable individual could be unable to place. Like Herzogovina.

Like those countries it had a prickly, overdeveloped sense of its own identity and insisted passionately on its need for independence. 'Independence?' his grandfather would roar. 'Vojvodina? It's like the Isle of Wight demanding independence.'

But Seymour's other grandfather, his mother's father, had died in an Austrian jail for Vojvodina's independence. And even his booming grandfather, who affected to deride petty nationalism, had been thrown out of Poland because of his devotion to it. It was part of their family history. Just as some families have a talent for gardening which crops up in different generations, so Seymour's family had a talent – or, possibly, the reverse – for dissenting politics.

It was a talent, though, that since their move to England they had tried to suppress. Seymour's mother never spoke about the past. His father wouldn't have anything to do with politics. His sister had switched interest to a different, non-nationalist kind of politics. And even Seymour's booming grandfather confined his interests these days to putting the world right with its newspapers every morning over the breakfast table.

Seymour had followed his father; and his avoidance of politics had been reinforced by his time in the police. For the average policeman, 'politics' was a dirty word. It was something those above were always involved in and best avoided. If in the course of your work you ran into it, you shied away. It closed off avenues, as it had done in Seymour's case when he had been looking at possible royal dimensions to the Jack the Ripper case.

What Seymour had come to see, though, over the last few days, was that politics was not always something to be avoided. It was not always something you could or should avoid. It was too important. Suppose Schneider was right? Or if his testimony was too tarnished, what about Lomax? Lomax, who had at first seemed such a dilettante – the al fresco Consul! – but who had gradually shown himself to

171

have an engagement with the world that was far from frivolous. Seymour was beginning to feel that he ought to know more about politics. Not to engage, no, but not to avoid, either. If politics was this important, you needed at least to be able to grasp what the hell was going on.

And what he was gradually coming to see, too, was that he did have a bit of a feel for such things. 'He'll be like a fish out of water!' the man at the Foreign Office had said contemptuously. Well, maybe. At first. But, actually, these waters were waters that Seymour knew. He had grown up in them, unconsciously been steeped in them. He knew about them from the inside. His mother's father had, after all, died in such currents. Some things you didn't have to learn: you knew.

And possibly, Maddalena, in her desire for knowledge, was making a similar progression.

She came to the Consulate later in the morning. Augstein showed her in.

'I hoped you would be here,' she said, as she came into the room. 'I wanted to tell you to look in at the piazza. It's all beginning to happen.'

'The Futurists? Marinetti's Evening? I thought that was tomorrow.'

'It is. But it's starting already.'

'At least it's starting. I wasn't sure that it would.'

'Oh, Marinetti's more competent than you think.'

'Is there anything to it, do you reckon? This Futurist business?'

'I ask myself that a dozen times a day. At one time I was convinced that there was. It seemed so exciting, so bold. So different. And Marinetti was so enthusiastic. I was rather swept away.'

'And now?'

'Now I am not so sure. Not so much about the art, I still think that's very exciting. But about the other claims. You know, changing the world and all that. I used to talk about

172

it with Lomax. He said that the world *was* changing. What with the new technologies of electricity and steam and oil, and that people would change with it. The question, though, was how people would use them. You know, to lead a better life, or just to make better bombs and bullets.'

'And what did he think?'

'He said it was a toss-up.'

She looked up at the pictures on the wall.

'And that perhaps what art was expressing was potential, what *could* happen, not what *would* happen. I don't know. Lately I have begun to think that art doesn't express anything at all. It is just marks on the wall. Perhaps I am getting tired of art. Perhaps it is time for me to move on.'

'What to?'

'Ah!' said Maddalena. 'That's the question.'

She was silent for a while, and sat there looking broodingly at her feet. Then she looked at him, almost defiantly, and said:

'Do you know why I go to the library every day?'

'You said you wanted to know about things.'

'Yes, I want to know why the Hapsburgs are so awful, and how it is that they can keep Trieste from us, and why it is that people like Lomax should die. I want to know why some should be rich while others aren't. But do you know why I want to know these things?'

'Why?'

'Because,' she said, frowning, 'I want to be in charge of myself. I don't want others to be, or things to be. If you were a poor woman from Puglia, you would understand.'

'I think I can understand.'

Before she left, he asked her to find out something for him.

'Is this for Lomax?'

'I think so.'

She nodded.

'Very well, then.'

*   *   *

173

Seymour sat at Lomax's desk, thinking. He knew he had it nearly all now, but there was still something missing, something that would put it all into place. He could see that the reception at the Casa Revoltella was central, but exactly why was it so central? The reception, with all Trieste's worthies there, the Chamber of Commerce, the consuls, the Governor –

And then he saw.

On his way, Seymour passed through the Piazza Grande. It was, indeed, as Maddalena had said, warming up. Although it was only mid-afternoon it seemed quite full. The tables in the cafés were practically all occupied and street performers of all sorts, jugglers, mimers, musicians and tumblers, were busy working them. In some places the musicians were giving impromptu concerts and one or two people were even dancing. There was a general air of suppressed excitement. By evening the piazza would be really buzzing.

Seymour's artist friends were, as might be expected, already at their table. They hailed him and he sat down, briefly, for a moment.

'Isn't that Boccioni?' said Luigi, pointing to one of the tables.

'And Severini?'

Seymour could see that the artists were impressed.

Marinetti suddenly shot past them.

'Hey, Filipo!' they called. 'How about a drink?'

'Can't stop!'

'Can't stop!' The artists' heads swivelled. 'Can't stop for a drink? Is something wrong?'

'Everything's wrong!' said Marinetti dramatically. 'We've only just been able to get into the Politeama. And nothing's there! No chairs, no bottles –'

'No bottles?' said James.

'The banners haven't arrived. The musicians, who were supposed to be there for rehearsal –'

'Why don't you just sit down, Filipo? Have a drink!'

'There is no time for drink. There is no time for anything! Everything has to be done!'

He strode off.

'No time for a drink?' said Lorenzo. 'If this is the Future, you can count me out.'

Marinetti suddenly came racing back.

'I need dwarfs!'

His eye fell on James and Seymour, both unusually tall, and moved on disappointedly. It lit on Ettore.

'Rehearsal!'

Ettore was dragged away, protesting.

Two men on stilts, dressed as giraffes, began to move through the tables distributing flyers for the Evening. As they passed one of the tables, a man leaped up and stroked them fondly. One of the giraffes sat down on his lap and lifted a leg casually on to the table.

'Lomax would have loved this!' said Luigi.

'Lomax,' said James, who had already clearly drunk far too much, 'was Irish.'

He looked around pugnaciously, as if challenging anyone to disagree with him.

There was a slight pause.

'Ye-e-s?' said Lorenzo doubtfully.

'He was *all right*,' said James, glaring round.

'Yes, yes.'

'He couldn't help being English.'

There was another slight pause.

'But I thought you said . . .?'

'I know that!' roared James. 'Do you think I'm daft? He was half Irish and half English. So he was both. Both!' he said triumphantly.

'We-ll . . .'

'He was half and half. Like a shandy,' he giggled.

'Like a . . .?'

'Shandy. An English drink, you ignoramuses. (Or is it ignorami?' he muttered to himself.) 'Half bitter, half lemonade. Or possibly ginger. Bitter is beer. The Irish half,' he said firmly, 'was the bitter.'

'Well, it would be.'

'The English half was the lemonade.'

'Very true.'

'Light, slight, blight – Blighty!' he said, with satisfaction. 'That's England for you. The English half,' he enunciated carefully, 'held him back. It made him a consul.'

'Poor Lomax!'

'The Irish half,' James roared, 'made him side with the underdog. It made him fight against injustice!'

'Good for him!'

'He was a man divided,' said James, beginning to weep. His head fell on to the table. 'Aren't we all?' he murmured.

'I know what I like,' said Kornbluth, 'and it isn't this.'

'Hadn't you better wait? It's not happening until tomorrow.'

'I don't need to wait. I know what those layabouts are capable of producing. Giraffes! And' – he lowered his voice – 'filth! I saw them this afternoon. When I was working out where I wanted to put my men. Naked women! Well, they weren't quite naked, there was a little star over – well, you can guess where. I wouldn't like my Hilde to see it, I can tell you. Fortunately, she won't be there. She wanted to go, when she heard the Governor's lady would be there, but I put my foot down. "Listen," I said, "I've got to put up with it, but there's no reason why you should." "It's the Future, they say," she said. "I'll tell you one thing," I said. "It's not going to be *your* Future! So, you're not going."'

'Are you tied up completely tomorrow with policing?'

'Pretty well. And that's another thing I've got against that lot. It's taking me away from what I should be doing. Why? Was there something else you had in mind?'

'I've found out something. In fact, I knew it before. Those Socialist strikers told me, but I've only just put two

176

and two together. When Lomax left the Edison that night, he didn't leave by the ordinary way. There's another door.'

'Another door?'

'Yes, Machnich uses it when he doesn't want to run into people who might be waiting outside. I think Lomax used it that night.'

'Where is this door?'

'It opens into the Piazza delli Cappucine. Could you get your men to check if anyone saw him come out? And if anyone was seen waiting for him.'

'I'll have them on to that,' said Kornbluth, 'right away.'

Seymour hesitated.

'There's one other thing. It's just possible that the men you might be looking for are two Herzegovinians.'

'Herzegovinians?'

'Yes. Posing as students. And staying, I think, in a student hostel.'

'I'll get someone to go round them.'

'You don't need to. I've got somebody already doing that.'

'You have?'

'Yes, that girl who was with the artists. Maddalena, her name is.'

'That troublemaker? But –'

'I think you might find her,' said Seymour, 'in the public library.'

'The library!' said Kornbluth incredulously.

Chapter Thirteen

'Signor Machnich to see you,' said Augstein.

'Ah!' Seymour rose from the desk. 'Signor Machnich! It is good of you to come.'

Machnich glanced round the room, took in the pictures on the walls and winced, then sat down.

'Signor Machnich, I have a confession to make. I am not a King's Messenger but an English police officer. I am here to investigate Signor Lomax's death. Now, I know you were a friend of Signor Lomax. I have found out some things that interest me, and I wonder if I could run through them with you?'

'Certainly,' said Machnich. 'We were people of a kind. Close together. Like that!' He put his two fingers together.

'Quite so. And that is why you, of all people in Trieste, can help me. Can we go back to the beginning? You got to know each other when he was advising you over that cinema business, and you got on surprisingly well. Not only that, you were a prominent Serb locally, so it was, perhaps, natural that he should talk to you when he found out something about the Serbs - that they were running an escape route through his Consulate.'

'Well, now –'

Seymour held up his hand soothingly.

'It's all right,' he said. 'Do not worry. We are talking about Lomax, yes? Only about him. He was not, I think, too disturbed. Indeed, he had some sympathy for the students. He may even have been prepared to let it con-

178

tinue, although I think he probably suggested to you that you should think about bringing it to an end. Anyway, he talked about it with you. Why not? You were people of a kind, you understood each other. And you were friends.

'And then, suddenly, you were not friends. Why was that, I wonder?'

He waited.

Machnich merely shook his head.

'Shall I tell you what I think? I think it was because you, or Rakic, misread the friendship. You thought it went further than it did. You put something to Lomax and he didn't like it. Not one little bit!

'But, again, you, or Rakic, misread the situation. You thought you could persuade him. You kept sending him to Lomax, or, perhaps, he insisted on going – he was that kind of man. But still Lomax wouldn't agree. And in the end Rakic realized that he would have to do what he wanted to do another way.

'The trouble was, he had a deadline. What he wanted to do could be done only on a particular occasion. He needed access to the reception at the Casa Revoltella.

'Well, Rakic being Rakic, he thought he could bluster his way in. Lomax, however, was there. He may even have been waiting for him, guessing that he might try to get in. Anyway, he intercepted him. There was a fracas at the entrance and Rakic was prevented from going in and delivering his package – which, incidentally, he claimed was for you. I don't think you would have been very happy to take possession of it. That was, perhaps, why you weren't there. And if that was so, then it means that you knew about it, didn't you, and what Rakic was intending?'

'I know nothing about that,' said Machnich, 'or any of it.'

'Don't worry. We're only talking about Lomax. For the moment. And Lomax, you see, had suddenly become important. For it wasn't just that he had stopped Rakic from doing what it was that he had in mind to do, it was

179

that he knew about it. He knew about it and could tell someone about it. Schneider, for example.

'Now why he didn't tell Schneider about it straightaway, I don't know. Perhaps he was so shocked by it, perhaps he didn't quite believe that it could happen, until he saw Rakic there. And then perhaps when he did, he still couldn't quite believe it. Or maybe that a man he looked upon as his friend could lend himself to such a thing. So he waited and thought about it. Perhaps, in the end, he was too much of a diplomat: too cautious, reluctant to move until he could be quite sure, could quite convince himself. That was his mistake.

'For Rakic, too, was thinking about it. He knew he had to act, and act quickly. Luckily, the two men he had wanted had now arrived and they were just the men for something like this.

'So he got you to ask Lomax to come and see you. In your room at the Edison. I don't know what the pretext was. Perhaps it was precisely this. To talk about what had happened and what he was going to do. He might even have told you that he was going to see Schneider and you might even have tried to persuade him not to.

'Anyway, afterwards he left. By your private, secret door. Was that your suggestion? I think it must have been. If so, it was hardly an act of friendship. Because outside the door Rakic's two men were waiting.'

'This is mere supposition,' said Machnich. 'I spit on it.'

'Is it? Is it supposition that Rakic tried to get into the reception at the Casa Revoltella? Is it supposition that he wanted to leave a package? That Lomax stopped him?

'That you invited Lomax to the Edison the night that he died? That he left not in the ordinary way but by a door which only you – or so you thought – knew about? And that he was killed after leaving that door?'

'It is mere supposition,' said Machnich. 'You cannot prove any of it.'

'I am not so sure. You see, Mr Kornbluth has learned about the secret door. And he has been checking with

180

people who were in the Piazza delli Cappucine at the time that Lomax would have come out of the secret door. And he has found someone who saw him come out. This person is prepared to say that he saw Lomax leave with two men. He is even able to identify the men. They are the two Herzegovinians whom you brought to Trieste and who were so close to Rakic that the strikers thought they were his bodyguards. The two men whom Rakic tried to get Koskash to make out papers for so that they could leave quickly and secretly. After they had done what they had been brought to Trieste for. He refused, and I hope that will be remembered in his favour.'

'Whatever your person in the Piazza delli Cappucine saw,' said Machnich, 'he did not see me. There is nothing to link me with any of this.'

'We shall see what the Herzegovinians say. Because, you see, we shall now have an opportunity of questioning them. Since Mr Kornbluth was able to find out where they were hiding and has arrested them.'

Machnich let out a long breath.

'Why are you telling me this?' he said.

'Because I hoped that you would save us a lot of time by telling me that you recognized it to be true.'

Machnich laughed.

'Do you think I would do that?'

'Well, yes, I think you might.'

'Well, let me tell you, you are wrong.'

'I think you might,' said Seymour, 'once you recognize that you have been used.'

'Used?' said Machnich.

'Used by the Bosnians. The Serbs here have been used by the Bosnians. And the intention was that Serbs everywhere should pay the penalty.'

'What is this?' said Machnich.

'You knew what Rakic intended to do. He intended to plant a bomb which would kill the Governor. But do you know why he wanted to do that?'

181

'To strike a blow at the Austrians. To hit back at them for their annexation of Bosnia.'

'Oh, yes, but it went further than that. Much further. You see, as Mr Schneider once explained to me, one thing is bound to another. One country is bound to another. Russia, for example, is bound by treaty to Serbia. So if Austria attacked Serbia for some reason, it would be obliged to intervene. Rakic, who was, of course, Bosnian, meant to supply that reason. He intended to kill the Governor and then see that Serbia was blamed for it. Why else, do you think, he associated himself so much with you?'

'Could this be?' said Machnich.

'He meant to slip out and leave you to take the blame. You, the Serbs.'

'Bosnians!' said Machnich, angrily. 'What can you expect from a people like that but treachery?'

'Why I am telling you this,' said Seymour, as Schneider and Kornbluth came into the room, 'is so that you can have a chance of putting things right. Rakic, fortunately, did not succeed. But the story will come out and it will anger the Austrians. You can see that the right story is told and that the right people are blamed. Not the Serbians.'

Machnich was silent for quite a long time. Then he said:

'I can do better than that. Because the story is not over. Rakic failed, but he is going to try again. The Governor will be at the Politeama tonight. With those crazy Futurists. In fact,' he looked at this watch, 'in just about twenty minutes' time.'

Huge, stridently coloured banners were draped all over the front of the Politeama. *The Future is Here!* they cried. *This Evening!* Balloons with bright faces painted on them hung over the doors. A gigantic papier-mâché mask had been hoisted into a central position among them. From its mouth dribbled a string of sausages. Was it Seymour's imagination, or just his weakness of aesthetic sense, or did

182

the mask faintly resemble the face that hung everywhere in Trieste, the Emperor's face beneath the familiar peaked military cap?

And at the doors, and everywhere round the Politeama, were policemen. They checked everyone who went in, opening all handbags and parcels, plunging their hands deep into the voluminous pockets of the cloaked worthies and the surprised, and resentful, Citizens of the Future.

'What have you got there?'

'It's my penis, isn't it?'

'Then why has it come off?'

The policeman's hand emerged from the pocket holding a banana.

'What's this?'

'It's for the performance. Hey, give it back!'

The policeman, slightly bemused, surrendered it.

'Thank you, officer. Would you like a bite?'

A cry went up.

'Hey, they're confiscating penises now!'

Marinetti came rushing out of the doors.

'You're ruining everything! Everything!' he cried to Kornbluth in anguish.

'I've told you –' began Kornbluth.

But Marinetti had already dashed back into the hall. A moment later he re-emerged with a large, hastily painted notice which he propped up against the doors. It said:

They are Trying to Arrest the Future!
Please Give them every Co-operation. Let them search your pockets.

The Citizens of the Future responded enthusiastically, pulling out their pockets for the benefit of the policemen. Some of them took down their trousers.

'Just bloody get on in there!' said Kornbluth, harassed.

Inside the hall huge backcloths on the walls showed aeroplanes diving, cities exploding, museums and galleries collapsing, fractured Venus de Milos tumbling out of them

183

in dozens, racing-cars hurtling off the walls, fireworks opening into golden raindrops which became shell bursts tinged with red, and military caps rising disembodied into the air as if suddenly levitated by an explosion, one of the caps instantly recognizable as that of the Emperor of the thousands of portraits, with a seagull poised ominously above it, about to jettison a load of white excrement, some of which had, indeed, already fallen.

Down one of the aisles strutted a large ginger cat. It was six feet high and had its arm around a nude girl. The nude girl was Maddalena.

Or nearly nude. She had put on a cat mask which covered her face; black, to go with the bow-tie she had donned. That was the only thing she had donned; apart, Seymour suddenly saw, from a tail.

'How do I look?'

'Well,' said Seymour, 'not overdressed!'

'How do I look?' said the ginger cat anxiously, in a voice that Seymour recognized. 'It's very hot in here,' James complained.

'Have you seen Rakic?' asked Seymour.

'He was standing here a moment ago,' said Maddalena.

Seymour scanned the audience and couldn't see him.

'Are you sure?'

'Positive.'

He looked around again. Over by the door Kornbluth was doing the same thing.

'Why?' asked Maddelena.

'It's important, We've got to find him.'

Marinetti came running down the aisle.

'Perfect!' he said. 'Take it up there.' He pointed towards the stage.

'I can't see in this!' complained James.

'I'll go first,' said Maddalena.

They stooped and picked up a long cardboard box. It was black. It took Seymour a moment to realize that it was a replica coffin.

The two cats, the ginger one and the black one, set off up

184

the aisle towards the stage. There was a little ripple of applause.

It was hard for them to find a space on the stage because most of it was already occupied by the two giraffes, dancers dressed in spangles and little else, a small group of bearded, slightly apprehensive poets, and, at the back, a row of even more apprehensive, mostly uniformed worthies.

There was a stir at the door. The police around it parted and in came a small group of clearly still more exalted worthies, led by a grand couple, he in gorgeous, be-medalled uniform, she in a beautiful, near-ballroom dress.

'I thought they'd been told not to come!'

'They insisted!' whispered Kornbluth.

The couple mounted the steps to the stage and took their place in the centre of the worthies.

'He was here!' Seymour whispered. 'Maddalena saw him.'

'Jesus!' said Kornbluth and started going up and down the aisles scanning the rows.

With a discordant fanfare of trumpets the Evening's entertainment began. A tall yellow banana marched to the front of the stage and bowed to the audience. It split apart and Marinetti emerged, to applause, dressed as a ring-master.

He cracked his whip and the dancers at once began cartwheeling and somersaulting. The poets all started to declaim their poems, simultaneously and increasingly loudly. Live fish were thrown slithering on to the stage. The dancers began to hurl them into the audience. The row of worthies, as goggle-eyed as the fishes, watched it all, stunned.

The two cats had put down their box.

Marinetti cracked his whip. He waited and then cracked it again impatiently. Maddalena gave the ginger cat a push and it started running round the stage in a circle. The dancers, still somersaulting, fell in behind it, and the giraffes behind them. Dwarfs, elves and gnomes emerged from the wings chased by an angry old troll, and joined the circling.

Kornbluth came back up the aisle.

'I can't see him,' he said, vexed. 'Are you sure?'

'It was Maddalena,' said Seymour. 'She seemed pretty sure.'

'He would have been searched,' said Kornbluth. 'Everyone was searched.'

'Where the hell is he?' said Seymour.

'Perhaps he's left,' suggested Kornbluth.

And then, suddenly, Seymour knew where he was.

'The Canal Grande! Send some men. He's catching a boat.'

Kornbluth, blessedly, didn't stop to question but spun on his heel.

Marinetti cracked his whip again and everything speeded up. The fanfares now were incessant. Crackers began to explode, the poets shouted louder and louder, the dancers leaped and jumped, chased now by the troll, who had transferred his attentions from the elves. He hurled himself on one of the dancers and began to surge with her in an ecstatic embrace. The music and the noise rose to a crescendo.

James, short-sighted, anyway, but also handicapped by the costume, blundered into the black box, tripped and nearly fell over. Maddalena caught him and pushed him back into the dance. She moved the coffin out of the way with her foot.

And then Seymour started running. Up the aisle and then up the steps on to the stage, pushing aside people, policemen and participants. He caught hold of the black box and began to tear at it with his bare hands, forcing the cardboard apart, so that he could reach down for what was inside.

He took it out and jumped down from the edge of the stage. He began to run up the aisle, pushing everyone aside.

186

'Signor, Signor –'

The police at the door half turned to stop him but he forced his way through them and out into the piazza outside.

It was dark but there were dozens of lamps hanging from the trees and from the front of the Politeama and by their light he could see people standing everywhere. The piazza was crowded. He looked around frantically.

And then there, at the end of the piazza, he saw that there were no people, just stalls dismantled from the market that normally occupied that end of the piazza every morning, and in a corner something hanging, perhaps a sheet left out to dry.

He threw the thing as far as he could, towards that end of the piazza, hoping that it would fall on the other side of the stalls and that they would deaden the force of the explosion.

And the next moment there was a light brighter than that of all the lamps hanging from the trees and from the Politeama and he found himself lying on the ground and only then was aware of the crack that had hurt his ears and of the acrid smell drifting across the piazza towards him.

Chapter Fourteen

Kornbluth took Seymour for a farewell drink in the little café on the Canal Grande. Schneider was not invited.

Relations between Kornbluth and Schneider had, however, improved.

'He thinks the sun shines out of my backside,' confided Kornbluth, 'since I managed to get both the Herzegovinians and Rakic.'

Kornbluth had got to the Canal Grande just in time. The boat, with Rakic in it, had already pushed out from the quay. Kornbluth, with surprising speed for so bulky a man ('But, then, I was always the fastest boy in the village, especially when the farmer was after me'), dashed along the quay, commandeered a boat which was itself on the point of departure, leaped aboard and directed it out into the canal where it blocked off the escaping boat until his men could get there.

The valiant *lamparetti*, displaying a zest for combat and a disregard for their uniforms hitherto unsuspected in them, hurled themselves into the water and into the fray and succeeded, by sheer weight of numbers, in seizing the vessel.

Rakic, chagrined but defiant, was not the man to deny his role in the affair, especially since he suspected that others were trying to belittle it. He attributed his failure solely to the weakness and treachery of Machnich.

'Never trust a Serb!' he said gloomily.

'Never trust a Bosnian!' retorted Machnich indignantly, when this was relayed to him; and both spilled all.

'Never trust a Serb *or* a Bosnian!' said the Italians, when they heard about the affair. 'Or a Herzegovinian for that matter.'

The artists were, on the whole, delighted by the outcome of the Futurist Evening, although they were judging its success purely in aesthetic terms. 'A landmark in Western art!' said Marinetti, very satisfied with the Evening and especially with himself.

James remained somewhat confused about the whole business, thinking to the last that Seymour's eruption on to the stage was merely part of the planned proceedings, and taking the explosion outside as one of Marinetti's accompanying fireworks.

Seymour, before leaving for London, had written to Auntie Vi asking if he might keep one of the pictures on Lomax's wall as a memento of the experience. Many years later he was astonished to find that the value of the painting was greater than the whole of his lifetime earnings as a policeman, even with the value of his house thrown in, but, then, Seymour had never really understood about art.

Maddalena had a number of sketches by the Futurists in her possession and the sale of these, later on, financed her further studies.

Seymour, dithering to the end about Maddalena, received some fatherly advice from Kornbluth.

'It's not that I'm not broad-minded,' he said, 'but it's not the sort of thing you ought to allow. Suppose I let my Hilde cavort around like that. How would it look?'

Not bad, Seymour forbore from saying.

'You've got to think of these things when it comes to a wife. *Kinder, Küche, Kirche*, remember. Children, kitchen, church. Now you can go easy on the church bit. Religion's all very well but some women go crazy about it. Children are important, they keep a woman out of mischief. But, in the end, the kitchen is the thing. What's she like at cooking?'

Seymour did not know. He thought it was probably not

something at which Maddalena excelled. However, he did not attach to it quite the importance that Kornbluth did. There were other qualities in Maddalena that attracted him.

But, then, how would his family take it? His mother? He chided himself. He was a grown man and what did it matter how his mother took it? Or the whole of the East End, for that matter?

He remained divided to the last and compromised by inviting Maddalena to come over to London and see the libraries.

He had some really tricky business to settle, though, before he left.

'I don't see how I can,' said Schneider. 'He has committed a crime, a very serious crime, and must face the consequences.'

'But he did refuse to help the Herzegovinians escape: and the information he provided was of very great value in leading to their and Rakic's detection!'

'We could exercise some degree of leniency, I suppose,' said Schneider.

Unfortunately, that did not extend to Koskash's immediate release and he had to stay in prison for some months yet. However, there was no longer any risk of him being physically ill-treated and, accepting that he had not behaved correctly, he was content with the outcome. Especially as his wife remained free.

Seymour's real battle over him came when he got back to London.

'Loyalty to one's staff is all very well,' said the older man doubtfully, 'but –'

'Not even his staff, strictly speaking,' the younger man pointed out.

'Well, then –'

'However,' said the younger man, 'the man seems to have felt a considerable degree of loyalty to the Consulate, or so Mr Seymour says.'

'Yes, but he Breached Trust.'

'How far was that his fault, and how far –'

'He was certainly not properly supervised,' said the older man, sniffily.

'Exactly! Working for a man like Lomax. I think Mr Seymour may be right, you know.'

'You mean – *not* dismiss him?' said the older man incredulously.

'Oh, yes. Dismiss him. The Austrians will expect no less.'

'Rightly!'

'But, then, when enough water has flowed under the bridge . . .'

'Reappoint him?'

'Well, he did manage the Consulate in Lomax's absence.'

And so, after a time, Koskash was able to return to the Consulate.

'I think Mr Seymour has done rather well,' said the younger man, 'all things considering.'

The older man sniffed.

'Quite well, yes. For a policeman.'

Seymour returned from the Balkans thinking rather more than he had done about international politics. But not enough. Three and a half years later war broke out, and it had its origin in a similar Balkan event. He wondered then if, supposing he had been able to see into the future, there was anything he could have done which might, somehow, have averted it, if he could have said, loudly enough: look, this is the kind of thing that could happen, the sort of thing, in a powder keg like the Balkans, that might trigger it off. Lomax was the one who had known it, feared that it might be coming. He had, in his way, tried to stop what might have turned into it. And Seymour had tried, too. They had, in fact, in their different ways, both succeeded. They had put out a spark. But it had only been in a particular case and for a time. They could do nothing

191

about the general conflagration. That had to be left to the diplomats and the governments, and they failed. The Balkans remained a powder keg waiting for a spark.

Could not anyone have foreseen? He asked himself that four years later as the parapets above his trench shuddered under the shelling of the Somme. And then he wondered if someone had. Could those crazy Futurists, with their apocalyptic visions of the future, have been right after all?